Praise for the Swimming Through Clouds Trilogy

"It is the rare author who can end an emotionally compelling trilogy with the same resounding truth from which it was formed, but turned inside out. In *Soaring through Stars*, Rajdeep Paulus does exactly that. Crafting her characters' inner growth at a believable and often heart-wrenching pace across the series, this final book extends an exquisite peace to hearts where extreme fear used to dwell. This series should be on the shelves of every American high school. *Soaring through Stars* is a beautiful, perfect ending to a truly exceptional series."
~ Serena Chase, USA Today's HEA blog, Author of The Ryn

"Rajdeep Paulus writes young adult fiction with a new kind of hero…Despair and cruelty haunt its pages. Raj's most heroic characters find the strength to be compassionate at moments when it would be much easier to stand by and do nothing."
~ Amazon Author Success Story

"Tough and touching, resilient and raw—Rajdeep Paulus has crafted a story of love and abuse with the deft touch of a master, and she never averts her pen from the realities that face far too many women and children."
~ Tosca Lee, NY Times Bestselling Author of Havah and The Books of Mortals series with Ted Dekker

In *Soaring Through Stars*, the final book in her trilogy, Rajdeep Paulus displays an almost magical ability to portray dark and haunting subject matter with her descriptively lyrical style. Her poetic prose not only manages to bring her characters' devastating struggles vividly to life, but also their singular grace and courage as they fight to wrestle hope from the rubble of epic loss, grief, and trauma.
~ Lisa Amowitz, Breaking Glass, Vision, and Until Beth (Fall 2015)

SOARING
THROUGH
STARS

RAJDEEP PAULUS

Birch House Press
Est. 2015

ISBN-13: 9780996180115
ISBN-10: 996180117
Cover design: Deepa Elizabeth Paulus

First printing 2015
Printed in the United States of America
Author represented by MacGregor Literary, Inc.

Birch House Press
Est. 2015

For my daughters, Hannah Angeli, Nitha Joyce, Lydia Grace, and Sarah Priscilla. This mom never tires of watching you each discover life, grace, and who you are. I love you, baby girls. First and foremost, these stories are for you.

I live in the in between. Between holding on and letting go. Hurt clings to me. Hope teases me. Home. I can't explain why, but sometimes, I just want to go home.

1

~Talia~

The concrete steps before me are as inviting as the climb up a volcano. I shake my head at the engravings above the door, promising "Liberty and Justice for All." Because I'm the girl familiar with more than a pocket full of broken promises. Clutching my blue satchel to my chest like a shield, I march forward, thinking of the contents that I meticulously packed last night: Chapstick, a water bottle, Post-its, and the stories of the women I met at the shelter. Each owns her story. Each told her story. It's my turn today.

"Talia Grace Vanderbilt." The boom of the gavel hits the judge's desk when the crowd rumbles and turns, searching for me. "Please come forward and take the witness stand."

I swallow a thousand islands and inch my way down the aisle, recognizing many faces. Teachers. Neighbors. Jaya, Ava, Nahida, Sunny—survivors living at Hope Now. Even Diana with her specks and hair tied back in that familiar messy bun. They're all here. But I'm searching for the one who gave me the courage to be here in the first place. Lagan. Where is he?

My eyes lock with my younger brother's in the second row. He's sitting next to a woman wearing a wedding veil, but Jesse shakes his head. What's he trying to tell me? Don't testify? Lagan couldn't make it? Dad's gonna destroy us, even here in the place where the truth is supposed to be on our side?

Then the woman next to Jesse lifts her veil. Mom! But...but...

"Talia!" The judge's voice thunders. "Take the stand or be held in contempt."

I move past the lawyers and the staring eyes of the jury, afraid to look at the defense attorney's table. But as I turn to sit down, he's right there, wearing his suit and tie, blond hair freshly trimmed, hazel green eyes piercing into me, a smug grin plastered across his face. Dad nods to me as he drags a single finger across his lips. In that tiny motion, he tells me to keep quiet. Family secrets are called secrets for a reason.

"State your name and relationship to the defendant, please." The words float past my ears like an echo, and the woman asking me taps her clipboard impatiently.

"Talia Vanderbilt. Daughter." Pulling at a lock of my long brown hair, I twirl it between my fingers, fighting the urge to pull it over and hide my lips. Broken and ugly, I feel like everyone in the courtroom stares at my lips.

"Do you swear to tell lies, the whole lie, and nothing..." The words fade like someone turned the volume down, and then I can see her lips move as she holds a book out in front of me, but I can't hear a thing she's saying.

"Wait, what?" I ask, but she's now motioning for me to put my hand on the book and swear, but I'm watching her mouth, and she's laughing. She's laughing at me.

"Talia." Dad's lawyer rises and moves inches from me. "Tell us a little about your childhood. Your days with Daddy. A time when Mom was still around. Wasn't it a wonderful life?"

"Objection." My lawyer screams the word I only heard in movies until today. "Counsel is leading the witness."

"Denied." I hear the judge say calmly, but I'm trying to look around Dad's lawyer for Mom. Her veil pulled over her face again, I think I see tears trickling down her cheeks, but I can't be sure.

"Go on then. Talia, tell us about your little girl years. How your father loved you. Treated you like a princess. Did everything a perfect dad would do."

"No. I mean. That's not…" I start to say, but I can't hear the sound of my words. I clear my throat and try again. "Lies—"

"A little louder, please." Dad's lawyer turns to face the jury. "So we can all hear."

"L- L- L-…" My throat tightens and I can see my father across from me. Smiling and nodding. Nodding and smiling. Lagan. I need you.

"Well, Talia, if you have nothing to say, why did you bother coming today? I'm finished. The witness is all yours." Dad's lawyer returns and takes a seat beside my father.

Rubbing my throat with my right hand, I try to call out to my brother who suddenly sits there shirtless, scars dotting his chest, like the burns run so deep, they pushed all the way through from his back. Jesse. Jesse. Look at my brother! I'm trying to scream. That's the childhood we had! But no sound again, and even as my lawyer steps up to the podium I sit behind, the woman

3

next to Jesse rises and begins to walk toward the exit, her veil trailing behind her. A veil trimmed with tiny red petals. Turned down, the petals appear as tear drops. Blood, red tears.

"Wait. Mom! Wait for me!" I hear the words in my head, but my vocal chords are frozen—my hand in the air goes unnoticed.

"Talia, don't you want to tell the judge and jury how your father treated you and your brother? Speak up. This is your last chance."

Hot tears stream down my face, and my hands cover my mouth as I bite down on my lips. No pain. Only blood. And then Mom turns around, and right before she exits the courtroom, she doesn't say, goodbye. Nor does she say, I love you. Instead, she lifts her veil, with tear-stained cheeks and a voice laden with despair, she says, "Why bother?" and leaves.

I scream, "Wait!" But only hear the screech of my voice in my head. I try again. Unable to produce sound, I leave the witness stand and dash down the aisle after Mom, the judge screaming, "Order! Order in the court!" behind me.

As I pull open the heavy courtroom door, all I can think is, I can't lose you. Not again. Not now. When I need my mother more than ever. Like someone resisting in a tug of war, the door yanks to a close before I slip through, shutting on my outstretched hand and crushing my fingers. Alongside my hope.

The sting of my hand hitting the bedroom wall awakens me. It was only a dream. Hugging my throbbing hand on this last morning in the shelter, I remind myself, "It was only a dream." On the actual day of the trial, everything will be worse. Far worse.

2
~Jesse~

I hold the door open for Talia. My room feels smaller
when two people walk in. "It's not much," I say.

Talia moves to the bed, sits down, and pats it, letting
her knapsack and satchel fall off her shoulder to the
mattress. "It's perfect."

"Fred says that he has a one-bedroom in another
building he owns that might open up next month, but
he's not making any promises." Fred's the landlord, a
no-nonsense, decent guy who smokes too much. Decent
enough not to give my room to someone else the three
weeks I was stuck in the hospital waiting for my kidneys
to wake up. A residual pain on the right side of my back
reminds me that I'm not one hundred percent yet, but
the doctor warned me that each ARF patient recovers at
a different rate. ARF is fancy for Acute Renal Failure.

Three weeks after Dad's arrest, Talia called me to tell
me she was ready to leave the shelter. Even though the
nursing staff told me I could use a week or so more of
R&R in the hospital, I promised Dr. Singh that I'd lie in
bed, and my big sister's the type to take care of
everything. What I didn't tell the doc was that my sister

already did that once in my lifetime, and I am never going back there.

I smooth my hair forward on top of my head. It's almost long enough for me to pull a few strands and see my black hair. After locking the door, I walk to the window. "The view's the best part."

"Really?"

"I was kidding," I say, when Talia makes to join me by the window. "There's nothing but wall and a tiny sliver of street here."

Looking back into my sister's hazel-green eyes that have always managed to match the shade of green she loves to wear, we exchange thoughts without words.

Can you believe Dad's in jail? Can you believe we're really here? Together? If Mom could see us now…

"I can sleep on the floor until we get a new place." I tap the wooden flooring, still leaning on the windowsill. "Can't be as uncomfortable as it looks, right? Plus, I hear in the Air Force, this would be considered luxury when you're on a mission."

"So you're going? After the trial? What about Summer?" Talia asks.

"Summer's great." Can't help but smile when I think about the girl who lent me her poncho on a rainy day and asked me to pay her back for ruining her poncho one churro date at a time.

Talia folds her arms over her chest as she sits back down on the edge of the bed. "I mean, won't you miss her?"

I haven't thought that far ahead. "I'll miss you more." These last few months were the best and worst weeks of my life.

Talia nods. Both of us went our own way for the first time. Separated but reunited again, I'm still so unsure of what the future looks like. But this feels good. Right.

"Freedom." Talia's word once hung in the air like a fused light bulb—one neither of us could reach to change. Until now. Until today. I go back to staring at the brownstone outside the window.

"Want to use the middle drawers for your stuff?" Hopping off the ledge, I slide the second dresser drawer open. "I can show you where the showers are, and maybe we can grab a bite to eat."

Talia's staring at me like I just spoke French. "Think you should take it easy still with your kidneys just starting to get better."

I pat my ribs. "I'm good as new." Dr. Singh did say to take it slow.

"Ummm. Last I recalled, your kidneys are behind you."

I turn around and around a few times, like a dog chasing its tail, stop, and say, "They're back there somewhere, and don't worry, T., I won't drop and give you twenty. Not this week, anyway."

Talia lies back on my bed and stares at the ceiling. "Can we just stay in and order a pizza or something?"

"Cheese? Or we could be really bad and get pepperoni? And a whole liter of Coke and have a burping contest." I raise my eyebrows twice. Dad would be mortified.

"Chicago-style deep dish with sausage and pepperoni from Gino's? Yes! Wait. Isn't that a lot of money?"

I wave off her question and call in the order with the phone Talia's boyfriend Lagan gave me, and as I tell the delivery person the apartment address, I watch Talia's eyes flutter to a close. We're here. We're safe. And we're together.

3
~Talia~

A little catnap till dinner arrives is all I need, the madness of the past few weeks has worn me out. Followed by the multiple meetings with Shelter personnel, social work, and Diana - the supervisor who became a friend, to make sure I left to a safe place. On top of everything, we had to make sure the restraining order against Dad took effect.

My mind U-turns away from my life to a road I'd rather travel down. The road where all the street signs are made of Post-its. And blue tulips line the pathways. And well, there's music. Because it's my dream. His hands outstretched to mine, Lagan is waiting to dance with me. I step forward, my feet floating as I close the gap between us, and just as my hand finds his, the music stops.

Bang. Bang. Bang. "Open up. It's the police."

Darting up from the bed, I look from the door to Jesse as I rise to my feet. My little brother backs up against the furthest wall from the door.

Through the peephole, I can see a male cop and his female partner standing there calmly. Maybe this has something to do with the restraining order against Dad.

As soon as the door opens, the male cop looks from me to Jesse. "Are you Justice Vanderbilt?"

Jesse nods.

Reading from a paper she just unfolded, the tall female officer says, "I have a warrant for your arrest. You have been accused of attempted arson and permanent damage to property. You are also being charged with theft and illegal possession of an armed weapon. We have the papers to search the premises."

What the heck? Do they mean what happened when Jesse and I left home?

Walking straight to my brother, the male cop tells Jesse to turn around and handcuffs my brother while saying, "You have the right to remain silent…" before joining his partner who didn't waste a moment before turning the room upside down.

Moving next to Jesse, I stand against the wall with him, but a piercing glare from the shorter, male cop discourages me from getting any closer.

After the cops search under the bed, in each of the dresser drawers, and dump the contents of my purse on the desk, they flip the mattress off the frame and tear the sheets and blankets off. Lady cop then pulls the desk drawer out and it comes crashing to the ground as Mister Policeman taps on the wooden flooring with his foot, listening for I don't know what. Shifting my attention back to Jesse, I see his eyes steel and his jaw tighten with every passing second. He stares at the open door like he means to make a dash for it, but his feet stay glued to the floor.

"Find anything?" Mr. Uniform asks his partner.

"Nothing." She cuts her eyes at Jesse. Then looks at me. "You're the girl from the YouTube video that went viral the night Gerard Vanderbilt got exposed, aren't you?"

She knows I am, and for a brief moment her glare softens, and I wonder if she feels sorry for me.

My insides cramp as the cops resume turning Jesse's organized little world into disarray. "What's gonna happen to my brother?"

"Doesn't mean he's not hiding it somewhere else?" Mr. Police Officer says, ignoring me as he speaks to his partner. "Let's take him down to the station."

A momentary taste of freedom dissipates with the sunset, no light streaming through the window now.

"I want to come with him," I say, shoving the items on Jesse's desk back into my satchel, my shaking hands causing me to fumble and miss the opening twice as I glance back and forth between my brother and my things. "Can I please go with my brother to the station?"

Female cop says, "You can follow in your vehicle or ride with him in the back."

We have no vehicle. "I'll ride with him," I say, and follow them out the door and down the stairwell.

"Little word of advice," Male cop says, facing forward but still talking. "Get yourself a really good lawyer. Chicago hates Gerard Vanderbilt and anyone who has anything do with him right now."

Jesse raises his eyebrows as we exchange a quick look. No one could hate Dad more than us.

The woman cop turns and says, "The apple doesn't fall too far from the tree, huh?"

Somewhere inside a wall goes up, graffiti sprayed across it with the words, "How dare you compare my brother to Dad?" but the words blur like I'm speeding by on a train with no brakes. Everything's happening so fast, I can barely get my bag over my shoulder.

A man with a cigarette hanging off his lip stops midway on the last flight of stairs as we pass him. "Oh no. I told you I didn't want any trouble. Get your crap out of my place by tonight. I warned you."

Jesse doesn't say anything, his head hanging low. And for a split second I mistake Fred's voice for Dad's and we're back home, and Jesse can't speak again.

"Fred?" He begins to rant on but I have no time. "It's all a big mix-up. Please give us a little time to clear this up."

Fred shakes his head, inhales from his cigarette, and blows smoke out of the side of his mouth. "I dunno."

The police have already moved ahead and out the door. I have to hurry if I don't want them to leave without me. I grip onto the railing as I stare at the exit.

"Please sir. We can't get kicked out now. Not when we finally...have a fighting chance." There's no time to wait for his reply. I rush out the door, swatting away at the tears that are starting to spill. Lagan. I need to talk to Lagan.

4
~Jesse~

The ice cold of the metal cuffs pinches my wrists as the male officer guides me into the squad car, and I'm looking all around to see if he decided to show up or just make his move from a distance. With the restraining order in effect, Dad has no choice but to attack from a distance. Like a calculated chess move, if Dad's check means to knock me out of the game, he has me confused for the son I once was. This game is far from over, and I have every intention of fighting back.

This is the second time in my life that I sit in a police car, holding back curse words as I stare at the police officer in the passenger seat. Mom sat in that seat during that first time. Years ago, the ride we took in the police car marked the one time Mom, Talia, and I tried to run away from Dad. But the police were on Dad's side and drove us right back to him. Doubt seeps in. Whose side are these cops on?

Chicago street lamps change from dim to bright, as the blinking squad car reflects in passing storefronts, and I remember the phone. "Left front pocket," I say, my voice lowered.

Glancing ahead again, the woman cop drives while the male officer fiddles with the radio. As Talia leans over to reach into my pocket, she pulls out the phone and some loose bills. My stomach grumbles, reminding me of a pizza I never got the chance to sink my teeth into tonight.

After tucking the money into her bag, Talia swipes the screen to find Lagan's number and texts him. I read the words in my head as they appear on the screen: This is Talia. Meet me at the precinct downtown ASAP. Please.

After pressing send, we exchange nods. The driver glances at me in the rearview mirror. Talia lays the phone down on her lap, and we both stare at it.

Minutes pass and the phone stays silent. *Come on, Lagan.* Text back already.

The car pulls into the station and still no word. Should we call someone else? Who else? When I step out of the car, the impending separation from my sister rakes across me like metal on pavement, and I slow my steps to linger near Talia, but the male officer's grip on my arm tightens. "Think you can pick up the pace? Some of us want to get home to our families tonight."

Seriously? He could care less that he's rushing me away from my only family. Then I remind myself that he's not the enemy and stop resisting the officer's directions.

"Will you be having counsel represent you when you make your statement or do you need us to provide you with a lawyer?" The officer behind the counter is asking me.

Shrugging my shoulders, I turn to face Talia so only she can see, and I mouth the words, I'm sorry.

"Wait. Luke!" Talia says.

Luke's the lawyer who helped Talia file the

13

restraining order against Dad. He also agreed to represent us in the upcoming trial against him.

After Talia gets off the phone with Luke, she tells me, "He's on his way," and helps me fill out paperwork.

The officer who brought us in says, "Say your goodbyes. I'll be back in two minutes to take Justice to his holding room."

The officer moves a few feet away, sits behind a desk, and begins to file papers piled in heaps on his tabletop. With limited privacy, Talia makes eye contact and nods. She's asking if I'm okay. I shake my head slowly. I'm nowhere near okay. Time passes too quickly. My heart sinks when Talia pulls me into a hug, my hands still cuffed behind my back. Like the time when I couldn't move, my sister does the holding.

"Talia," I whisper into her shoulder, and then under my breath, I say, "If he makes me goes to jail, I'll find him in there. And kill him."

Talia lets go, gripping her fingers into my shoulders. "No," she says. "We can't go back. Don't you dare send us back there. Lagan will help us. As soon as he—"

"Time's up." The officer takes me by the arm and as we part, I feel Talia's fingers quickly tuck something into my front pocket.

As I steal glances at my sister, I attempt to diffuse the volcanic anger rising inside me. This is not the time. I have to think about how to protect her. Who will protect her if I'm in here? *I'm counting on you, Lagan.* Wherever you are. I'm counting on you.

5

~Jesse~

Ushered to a room where an ink pad graces the table in front of a redheaded male officer, I can sense what's coming next. As the officer who walked me here removes my cuffs, the redhead motions for me to take a seat while he fills out paperwork. Thinking back, I suppose the whole setting-the house-on-fire wasn't such a smart idea, but when rage screams through your veins, reason gets lost in a whisper.

What ticks me off at this very second is Talia out there. And I'm in here. If something happens to her while I'm behind bars, I have no problem hurting Dad and spending the rest of my life blaming reason for preventing me from doing it sooner.

"Face forward." The photographer places a black sign in my hand before snapping the shot. Then a second of my side portrait. Taking the black board, he motions to the desk with ink pads on it.

"Right thumb first." The guy taking my fingerprints has his eyes glued to the sheets in front of me. "Press firmly into each box, but don't shift your hand."

I comply. And with each press, I imagine Dad's thumb pressing a lit match into the skin on my back.

After handing me a wet napkin to wipe off excess ink, he says, "Empty your pockets please." The officer now holds an opened bag with my name marked on it. "Everything will be returned to you when you leave."

Pulling out old receipts, my apartment key, and some loose change out of my right pocket, I place them into the bag.

"Your other pocket?" The guy does not look amused. I suppose he's done this long enough, he won't believe me if I tell him it's empty.

Reaching into my left pocket, I run my thumb and forefinger along the tiny square packet, regretting picking it up from a diner last week with a mint. I've been carrying it around ever since. The only other thing in there is a Post-it Talia shoved into my pocket. I haven't even read it yet.

"Any day now." The man's patience runs thin as I pull out the contents and try and fit my whole hand deep into the bag before dropping the book of matches and Post-it in, but he opens it wider and a humph leaves his lips. "Sure that's it?"

I nod, and because he's holding the bag open under my nose, I catch a glimpse of Talia's Sticky Note message, upside down, but the writing's clearly visible: Not letting you go, ok. Not now. Not ever. T.

I'm supposed to be saying those words to you, not the other way around. Cursing Dad under my breath, I look away from the man and the bag. And just when I think the cop is done with me, he opens up a chart and asks me some questions:

"Is there anyone who needs to know you're here?"

I shake my head. Talia is all I have, and she came

with me.

"Is there anything you're allergic to? Something that might cause you to have an anaphylactic reaction?"

Dad. But I suppose he means food. I shake my head no again.

"Last one: Is there any reason to believe you might hurt yourself?"

There was a time. One time. Clearing my throat, I say, "No."

"So, do we need to worry about you while you stay with us?" He repeats, clicking his pen on and off.

"No." I have plenty to live for now.

6
~Talia~

I pace up and down the hallway by the entrance wondering how long this whole mess will take to clear up.

"Talia! Is that you?" Lagan's cousin Rani walks toward me with a tall guy next to her. How'd she find out I was here? I've only met her once.

"Where's Lagan?" That's all I really want to know.

"You don't know?" the African-American-looking guy standing next to her asks. Or maybe he's Latino. "He's. Already here."

Maybe Rani sees the confused look on my face. "This is Reggie, Lagan's roommate. Lagan texted us to come down to the station."

I'm still not following. "They just arrested my brother Jesse."

Rani spells it out. "They got him too, huh? Lagan's been arrested," Rani says, her voice lowered. "I thought that's why you were here."

Jesse's phone buzzes in my pocket. The caller ID says, Unknown, and Lagan's voice streams through. "Hello?"

"Lagan?" I'm looking for him—across the room, past desks, phones ringing, and officers filing cases.

"They gave me one phone call besides my lawyer. I'm so glad you answered."

Turning away from Rani and Reggie to face the back wall, my small attempt at privacy proves unsuccessful when Reggie walks around and says, "We're gonna sort this whole thing out, don't you worry." He pulls the top off his water bottle and takes a swig, and I step a few feet away from him.

"I texted you from Jesse's phone. Why didn't you answer?"

"They took my phone when they took my fingerprints."

Imagining my brother going through that, I say, "They arrested Jesse too."

"I figured as much with the charges being about that night." Lagan pauses, then adds, "I wouldn't change a thing. I'm glad I went after your brother."

I'm a dam about to break, but Lagan's shoulder is nowhere nearby. "Let's just drop this whole thing. That's what my dad wants," I say, biting my lower lip.

"Shhhhh."

Closing my eyes, I imagine feeling Lagan shushing me gently in my ear.

Lowering my voice, I say, "I just know him. He's not gonna stop until we—"

"I know it looks bad, but you said no more running. We said, no more running."

"But your future. Your career. You need a clean record, right?" I won't let Dad dash Lagan's dreams.

"What?" Lagan chuckles. "My girlfriend thinks I'm guilty? And I haven't even been on trial yet!"

"Not like that." I quip back. "I just... What's the point?"

"Promise me," Lagan says.

I shake my head, but say nothing on the phone. All bets are off when it comes to Dad.

"Please." Lagan presses. "Promise me you won't back down. We'll fight this. Together."

7

~Jesse~

All those reruns of Law and Order I watched when I was stuck on the bed unable to move should make this night predictable if not familiar. What I couldn't have prepared for is the question in the eyes of everyone watching me walk by—what did *you* do to break the law?

Sure, we live in a country that brags of innocent until proven guilty, liberty and justice for all, blah blah blah, but let's be real. When I'm being escorted through the precinct from fingerprints to the holding room, the haters think I can't hear their jabs.

"Wonder where he got his values from?"

"Someone forgot to tell him that you don't follow in your father's footsteps if your dad's walking off a cliff?"

And the one most repeated: "Like padre like hijo." Ummm... we're Indian and South African, not Latino. But whatever. I get it. They think I'm like my dad.

The room I'm lead to is bare besides a desk and three chairs. "Someone will be here in a minute to talk to you. Stay put." And then the officer leaves me, locking the door.

The grey walls must be part of their tactics. Make a person imagine having to stare at these walls for weeks on end, and I'll bet confessions start dripping like leaky faucets. I don't need any motivation other than Talia. What can I say to convince the cops that I don't deserve jail time? Should I lie and say I never intended to set the house on fire? Should I show remorse for that day when I let my anger get the best of me? Or should I just twiddle my thumbs and act like I know nothing?

A knock at the door leaves me no time to decide. "So you're like the sequel to a bad book, huh?" A white male with a receding hairline and his green tie off-centered fails to introduce himself, but keeps talking as he closes the door, walks forward and leans over the desk across from me with his palms flat. "One Vanderbilt leaves and another replaces him. Looks like we won't even have to change the sign on the cell door."

One leaves? I rise and run to the door, but it's locked. "Let me outta here!" I bang repeatedly, my fists throbbing.

With my forehead pressed against the metal exit, I hear Mr. Crooked Tie say, "You're not going anywhere so you may as well sit back down. We need to talk."

I stay put. Then he says more forcefully, "Sit your arse back in the chair or I'll call for backup."

Teeth clenched, I walk back, lift the chair with both my hands and slam it down on the cement, then sit down with my arms crossed over my chest. Not for comfort, but to keep from swinging a punch at the cop who brought me the news about Dad being free.

"Your cooperation is appreciated," he says, and takes a seat across from me. "My name is Officer Barry Stetson, and I've been assigned to your case. Let's just make a few things clear right from the start. I'm here to get the truth. And I don't have time to waste on any more childish antics."

I refuse to look up at him.

"So let's just get a few basic questions out of the way so I can get your statement and move this case along." Officer Barry sits back with his hands behind his head. "Why would you want to set your house on fire? Was there some girlfriend you had plans to run away with? Were you pissed off at the paint your mother chose for your room? Do you prefer to camp? Because that's a great place to build a bonfire legally, son."

I can't tell if this guy really wants answers, or if he's just a natural jerk. I'm sure he did some stupid things when he was young.

Like he read my mind, Barry says, "Yeah, I chased a few cats up a tree. Stole a pack of gum from the corner store. And beat up a bully after school when no one was looking. The difference between you and me, son, is you got caught. And all it takes is one bad decision and you're done. Didn't your dad teach you anything useful?"

Didn't your dad teach you how to talk to people with a little respect?

Answering his own question, Barry says, "Well obviously you seem to think that some people are above the law. Is that what your daddy taught you?"

I look to the exit door, angry that I can't will it to open. Who's gonna keep Talia safe when Dad's out there? Lagan better come through for her.

"And then there's your partner in crime. Did he convince you to steal the gun? And stash it somewhere safe until you decide you want to commit another crime?"

"Partner?" I ask, confused by the last statement.

"Lag-an. Logan. Whatever his name is. We're gonna

get the truth from you boys one way or the other. Too many innocent people have died at the hands of punks who don't know how to handle fire arms, and we're not gonna let a couple of young hoodlums be the next two to take over the five o'clock news with blood on their hands. Look at this visit as a favor, son. Be glad we didn't find the gun, and be glad you didn't shoot it. Doesn't mean you're innocent or free to go. We still have the nonsense with the arson charges. When do you plan to fess up so we can save the taxpayers from another unnecessary trial?"

My head's spinning as I reach for the table to steady myself. "What do you mean? Did you arrest Lagan too?"

"What? Now you want to put in a request for a roommate in prison? That's already been decided. Accomplices to a crime never share a cell."

Luke. Talia said something about Luke coming. "Can I see my lawyer, please?" I need answers. How long am I stuck in here? Isn't there some sort of option for bail? Maybe the money I saved up from working for Jimmy will get me outta here. But more than anything, all I can think about is Talia.

Officer Stetson rises from his chair and walks back to the exit, talking as he leaves. "You disappoint me, son. With a name like Justice, don't think they'll go easy on you at tomorrow's bail hearing. Unless you've got a lot of green stored under your mattress, you're looking at a cozy cold corner in a cell till your trial. I'll be seeing you later. You can count on that."

And with those words, someone buzzes him out and I'm alone again.

Left alone to scream silently: *Talia! Run!* Get as far away as possible.

8
~Talia~

Reggie and Rani are chatting with the officer who walked Jesse through registration when I return from talking on the phone with Lagan.

"Your brother's in the room with his lawyer," the cop says to me, then turns and keeps talking with Reggie and Rani.

Shouldn't I be in there with him? I'm realizing the likelihood that my brother's coming back and we'll walk out of here together is about as likely as reversing time.

I start to ask: "How many days—?"

"I got here as soon as I could." A man wearing a three-piece suit and carrying a laptop case on his shoulder barges in on the conversation. He glances at his phone and then back to the Rani. "Where is he?"

Rani embraces the man and says something inaudible to him.

"Are you the counsel representing Logan Desai?" a woman carrying a clipboard approaches and asks.

"Yes." The man who has a faint resemblance to Lagan with his milk chocolate skin and head full of black hair says. "And his name is La-gan." The man turns to face Rani and says, "I'll catch up with you after on the phone. This could take some time. And don't worry, okay?"

"I'll take you to see your client." The officer leads Lagan's lawyer off in another direction and the whirring of the phones, clicking of keyboard keys, and laughter off to the side by some officers make me worry more. No one seems to care that Jesse was arrested. No one's telling me what will happen next.

When the woman with the clipboard returns and ushers us toward the waiting room, I ask, "Will someone please tell me what's happening to my brother? Can I see him?"

Before answering, she pulls several sheets off her clipboard and hands them to each of us. "This should answer all your questions, and if there's anything else, their lawyers can go over things with you. If there's something pressing, feel free to run your concerns by the information desk near the entrance, but understand that no one's delaying any help to you on purpose. We're very busy in here."

Rani turns into the waiting room, dabbing her eyes with a Kleenex I now notice in her hands. Reggie follows, but I detour to look for a restroom. I want to read these sheets where I can be alone. I spot the ladies' room and start skimming the FAQ section to learn, "What to expect when you or a loved one is arrested."

After skimming the first page, I can think of three questions that these papers don't address. For starters, how does a sibling know for sure her brother is okay in there? What if someone tries to hurt him? And can he request a cell next to a friend?

Following signs for the Information Desk, I stop short a few feet away, lean against the nearest wall and finish reading. I'll gather all my questions before I walk up to talk to somebody.

"Amit Shah would be so proud of both of you."

The voice makes me drop the papers, and I taste the blood in my mouth as I attempt to pull my sleeves down. Dad's standing a few feet from me, carrying a plastic bag with his name across it, wearing the same suit he wore the day he was arrested, his chin covered with a mostly grey beard.

I look past Dad, eyeing the two officers behind the info desk, near enough to call if he gets any closer.

Avoiding his eyes, I know I shouldn't trust him, but I recognize the name, Amit Shah. Mom's father. My grandfather. "You talked to him?"

"I wish I could. It's too late now." A smirk replaces Dad's sorrowful expression.

"What do you mean?" I try to step back, but my feet feel glued to the floor. Dad doesn't move either, but his words pierce like arrows shot into a hot air balloon. The balloon I rode in before this day started.

"Talia, Talia, Talia. Didn't you read about the flash floods Kolkata faced this monsoon season?" When I don't answer, he continues. "They wiped out entire villages, including the village your mother was from."

"Move along, Mr. Vanderbilt. You're free to go. So go." The older officer at the info desk pushes his chair back and stands with his arms crossed over his chest.

"That's right. When you're free, it's a sweet thing. Very sweet." Dad's smile makes my stomach churn.

"Officer…" I grit my teeth to keep from stuttering, but the word "help" gets stuck in my throat.

Dad lowers his voice to a whisper. "Come home, Talia. I can make this all go away if you just come home."

I shake my head as my feet lift like weights, but when I step backward, my heels meet the wall behind me.

27

"Mr. Vanderbilt, I suggest if you don't want to return to your cell, you move along." The officer walks over and stands between us with his back to me. "Your bail has been paid, and this can easily be turned from a chance encounter to a clear violation of your restraining order. Even if she arrived after you. Leave. Now."

"Look on the bright side." Dad gets his last word in as he pushes open the exit door. Before the door shuts behind him, he says, "At least your mother got out."

Did she? I want to ask out loud. We all know she's not here to answer the question for herself. And as Dad walks away, knocking the wind out of me, I'm the hot air balloon diving back to Earth, because just when I thought I was free, he still holds the string.

9
~Jesse~

When Luke arrives in the small room, his smile exposes the clear braces Talia told me about, making him look like a teen who greyed early.

"Luke Barrons, pleased to meet you." Luke holds his hand out to shake mine and if his grip is any indication of how he handles his cases, I'm glad he's on my side.

"What do I need to do to get out of here?" The neon exit sign above the door births a new hatred for the color red.

"That's what I'm here for." Luke opens up his laptop case and pulls out a Mac as he takes a seat across from me. "Let's get all the formal stuff out of the way and just so you know, I've asked Lagan's lawyer to step in so we can collaborate our efforts. Okay?"

I nod and begin answering Luke's questions. The ones I know the answers to, because there are a lot I don't. Like mother's year of birth. Mother's cause of death. Mother's occupation. And mother's mental and physical history.

"What about your father?" Luke says.

"What about him?"

"Date of birth."

"The worst day in the world."

Luke clears his throat. Then asks, "Occupation?"

"To torture his children."

Luke stops typing and looks me in the eye. "Any mental illness that you're aware of."

"All of them."

Luke shuts his laptop screen, folds his arms over his chest and says, "Describe your relationship with your father. Would you say that it was so bad it warranted trying to set the house on fire? Were you in any imminent danger? Were you trying to destroy him by destroying his property or were you …" Luke pauses, then says, "Planning to stay in the house while it burned down?"

"No!"

"Isn't that why you took the gun? To end it all if the fire didn't do the job?"

"No. Definitely not."

"Are you sure about that, because…" Luke scoots his chair closer to the table before saying, "I could make a very strong case for a young man who was pushed to attempted suicide by an extremely abusive father. A jury would believe it. I'd even place my bets on a unanimous vote to let you go. With some mandatory visits to a psychologist scheduled in of course."

Whose side are you on? "For the last time. No." I will not play Dad's games. I'll find a way to win, but do things my way. "I never set the house on fire. I never shot the gun. I don't even have it. Doesn't that help?"

Luke opens his laptop again and types something. "What were you thinking on that day? The day the charges refer to?" Luke's looking at his screen.

I take a deep breath and remember the conversation I had with Talia the morning we left home. "We, my sister and I, we needed an out. A way that Dad would never, ever, find us. So…I thought if we faked our deaths in a house fire… I thought we'd finally be free." There. I said it.

Luke's typing fingers stop and a knock at the door precedes an officer entering.

"Did you request a second counselor at this time?"

"Yes. Is he here?"

"He stepped away, but he asked me to make sure you had enough time with your client before he joined you."

"Yes. Please send him in when he returns."

When the door shuts, Luke's eyes dart back and forth as he re-reads his notes. Then he looks up and says, "I need you to think hard about what freedom means to you. Then we'll talk about options."

10
~Talia~

Walking back, my hands still feel jittery as I enter the waiting room, the smell of stale furniture permeating the air even when I sit near an open window. The sounds of busy Chicago streets below fill the air, and I can't help but wonder if he really left or if Dad's lurking outside there waiting to swallow me up in some dark alley.

"Lagan never stops talking about you," Reggie says, moving to a seat next to me. "It's great to finally meet you. Even though, I mean, of course, I would have preferred TGIF's or something a little more friendly than the police station."

"I know, right." Rani forces a smile as she joins us by sitting on the other side of me. "Anyone up for a vending machine run? I need chocolate. Asap."

"I'll find us snacks if you two wanna talk?" Rising from his seat, Reggie stops himself and sits back down. "You look like you just saw a ghost."

More like a monster. I grip one hand in the other to keep them from shaking, my stomach rumbling as Dad's words replay in my head over and over again. *Come home. Talia. Come home.*

"Should we leave you alone?" Rani asks.

But I can't answer. The words sour my mouth. *Come home, Talia. Come home.*

"We should give her some space." Reggie inches away from me. Rani returns to the other couch.

It's not his fault. Or Rani's. I know they're trying to be friendly and supportive. I feel carsick, like the room's moving. "I think I'll get some air," I say, and rise to walk back toward the restroom.

"I know this can't be easy for you," Reggie says, following me now. "Lagan and your brother, Jesse. This mess. Can I just say one thing?"

Exhaling, I look down the hallway and back to Reggie. "Can we talk when I get back? I just need..." and it's too late. The smells and sounds of the police station get the best of me as my eyes spot a trashcan and I vomit today's lunch of peanut butter and jelly and lemonade. Definitely did not want to taste them again.

Feeling a hand rubbing my back, Rani presses paper towels into my hands. "I'll walk with you to get some air. Just in case you...need a friend."

"Meet you ladies back here in a few," Reggie adds before slipping away. "Text me if you need me sooner, okay, Rani. I gave you my number, right?"

Rani looks down at her phone. "Lagan gave it to me earlier tonight. Will do."

As I finish wiping my mouth, I realize I can't exactly leave these contents in the hallway like this. Tying up the bag lining the bin, I carry it with me to the bathroom. Rani waits outside the ladies' room, and when I emerge, her eyes ask if I'm okay with her staying with me.

"Oh, Miss!" The same officer from the info desk catches my attention. "Don't worry. He won't be bothering you anymore. He'll be arrested immediately if he sees you outside this building and fails to comply

with the R.O., okay. If you have any doubts, just dial
911 immediately, okay?"

Feeling for the phone in my satchel, I repeat the
numbers to myself. 911. And as I make my way to the
exit, Rani follows me, shaking her head. "Was he talking
about your dad?"

I don't answer, but she does.

"Holy cow. He was talking about your dad. Your dad
did all this, didn't he?"

This? This meaning getting Lagan and Jesse arrested?
She knows the answer to that question. What she
doesn't know is how he's done so much more.

As we walk out to the street, Rani trails a smidgen
behind me. Stepping to the right, my pace quickens, as I
imagine invisible hands reaching for me. *Come home,
Talia. Come home.*

I know I'm running when my bag bounces against
me with every pound of the pavement. Into the night,
across streets, dodging pedestrians, people walking their
dogs, and vendors rolling their stands home for the
evening. Never looking back, I run and run until I hit
Lake Michigan. Panting and leaning on the back of a
park bench, I turn and look for the first time. Dad's
nowhere in sight. Rani didn't follow me. It's just me and
the water. And a few stars.

I'm here if you need me, a voice inside reminds me. I
lower my head. I know. I believe you, I tell the gardener,
my invisible friend whom I met under a broken down
willow tree—the place I first told someone how broken
I was myself.

I just... I don't know how much more I can take. If there
was a way to know how it would all turn out, but I know
that I'm asking for the impossible.

That's where you're wrong. Ask. For the impossible.

I want. I want to believe you. Walking along the

rocks, I imagine the night Jesse tried to walk on water, nearly sinking to his death. I think of all the days Mom took us to the beach back in Benton Harbor. The night we tried to escape and Jesse and I stopped to make sand angels in the midst of the madness. And then I know what I want. And what I want to ask for.

Asking in a room somewhere inside me where I know he hears me, I say, "Could you please send angels to watch over them? While this all gets sorted out." Especially, Jesse.

What else? The nudge comes as a surprise, but it's like he knows I'm holding back. *What do you want for you?*

No one's ever asked me before. It's always been about Mom. About Jesse. About keeping us from Dad's claws. And even as I stare out at the moon on the water, I know what I want most. The word leaves my lips like a secret, coming out of hiding.

"Courage."

11
~Talia~

Stomach a little settled, I pull my sleeves over my hands and turn to walk back to the precinct, knowing I should apologize to Rani for running off. I pull out the cell phone Jesse left me with and dial 911, but stop one press short of hitting send. With my hand on the phone and the other holding onto the blue heart pendant Jesse gave me, I make my way back, and even if Rani and Reggie left, I need to be near my little brother.

When I enter the waiting room, Rani's shaking an M&M packet upside down into her hand, and next to her, Reggie looks up from his phone and rises from his seat to hand me a can of soda he picks up from the end table. Ginger ale.

"Thanks," I say, and sit down on the opposite couch, placing the cold soda by my feet.

Rani takes a shot at the wastebasket with her wrapper and misses, then gets up to throw it out. She hasn't said a word to me.

"I'm...ummm..."

"Forget it." Rani dismisses my apology, but the less than warm tone of her voice suggests she took my shotgun sprint to the lake personally.

Reggie ignores the obvious tension in the room as he sits back down, but leans forward with the info sheets in his hands. He might be taller than Lagan. "According to these, there's really nothing for us to do here. I mean, we can wait. There's nowhere I have to be, so I'm happy to wait with both of you."

"You don't have to wait for me," I say.

A few moments pass with no one saying anything. Then Rani moves to the window, looks out, and turns back.

"Maybe you're used to doing things on your own," Rani says, her arms crossed over her chest, "but if we're gonna help these guys, it could help if we work together. You know what I'm saying?"

Resisting the urge to bite my lip, I know she's right. I learned that in the shelter. The women there came together and were there for each other. We were stronger because of it.

"I'm sorry." I have to say it to clear the air. "I just needed to run. So...I would remember I chose to stop running." I'm looking at Lagan's friends, but I'm not expecting them to understand.

Rani turns back to look out the window, but Reggie exhales, moves to stand in front of me and holds his hand out. "Hi. My name is Reginald George Montgomery the Third, but my friends call me Reggie. Born and bred in Hotlanta where there's always room for peach cobbler and a plate of hot wings. Pleased to meet you."

As I shake Reggie's hand, I feel my tightened stomach muscles relax for the first time all evening. The whole starting over reminds me of those early days with Lagan and why these guys are friends. Rani's arms drop to her sides before she joins us, sitting beside me, her shoulder nudging into me. "And I'm Rani, Lagan's cousin. We've known each other since we were in diapers." Her eyes remind me of Lagan's.

"Sorry to interrupt," Lagan's lawyer stands in the doorway. "But can I have a word with Talia?"

"Dad!" Rani says, rising to greet him. "Is Lagan okay? Please tell me everything's gonna be okay?"

He answers the question with a hand up, motioning for me to follow him, and as we walk just outside the door, he introduces himself as David Desai, Esquire. "Oh and that's Devid with an e. Sorry, we had to meet like this. Lagan has mentioned how fond he is of you."

I force a small smile.

"I'm sorry to introduce such a sensitive matter, but Lagan wanted me to make sure you have a place to stay tonight. He doesn't want you to be alone, and my wife and I would be more than happy to have you until things settle down."

I hadn't thought that far ahead, but I suppose they might not let me sleep here tonight. I guess I should have some options.

"How 'bout you take my number and call me if you decide to stay with us. Rani will bring you home." Mr. Desai adds, "And Beta, we're late birds, so don't worry how late it gets. Just call us."

"Thank you," I say, but I have questions that have nothing to do with where I'll sleep tonight. "What's gonna happen to Lagan and my brother? When can I see them again? Or talk to them? Can I talk to my brother to see if he's okay?"

"I'm going in to discuss what happened with your brother and his lawyer. Your lawyer will give you the update as soon as he is finished, I'm sure. I just didn't want to miss you since Lagan was most concerned about you. But to answer one of your questions, the boys will spend the night here, and at the bail hearing tomorrow, the judge will decide if they can leave based on their word, or if they need to post money to ensure they will show up if this case goes to trial."

Money? "How much money do you think they'll ask for?"

"This will all be determined tomorrow, but Talia, the best thing you can do for your brother is to rest." And with that, he pokes his head into the waiting room and adds, "You kids go home and rest. Nothing to be done till the morning. The bail hearing is scheduled for 9:00AM. I'll talk to you soon, okay?"

"But you said my lawyer will come out to talk to me." I look over his shoulder, but there's no sign of Luke.

Devid looks at his watch. "He's sure to ring you up when he's done in there. Regardless, nothing will change tonight, and no one's allowed to visit with Lagan or Jesse at this point."

My heart sinks, and I don't even know if Jesse read the Post-it I slipped him.

"At least get yourselves something to eat," Devid says. "And Talia, call me. Anytime, okay?"

I nod, close my eyes and ten more questions come to mind, but when I open my eyes, he's gone.

12
~Jesse~

Another knock at the door announces Lagan's lawyer's arrival. The man marches up to the desk and lays his hands on his papers. He's still standing. "My client will plead not guilty at the arraignment. And you, Counsel?"

"Please, call me Luke." Luke motions to the empty chair and he sits next to Luke.

"And call me Dev."

"Jesse will also plead not guilty." Luke lowers his screen without shutting his laptop. "But, I'm afraid the bail will be set pretty high after the arraignment, because the attempted arson charges fall under criminal rather than simple civil disobedience."

I'm about to ask how high is "pretty high," but Dev speaks up first, shaking his head. "These boys are too young to be spending time in jail. I can call the judge in the morning since they both have clean records, and this is considered a first offense. Push for a promise to show up in court rather than any bail amount."

"But would your client need to stay here if a bail is

set? Does he have funds available to him?" Luke looks confused.

"I guess you haven't had a chance to get to know my client." Dev looks at me like we're exchanging a private joke. "Lagan chooses to stay if your client has to stay."

So I won't be alone. Classic Lagan. Doing what he knows would mean the world to Talia, even if it means he's separated from her.

"Legally, I am obliged to tell you all your options." Dev looks directly at me now. "And the biggest card on the table is that the opposition suggested mutual cooperation to, in his own words, 'make this all go away.' Even though technically, the only way cases like this or the upcoming one where your father's on trial get thrown out would be if key witnesses refuse to testify. In other words, no evidence, no case."

Luke and Dev both stare at me, waiting for me to say something.

I'm nodding to the table.

"No," I say, pushing away from the table. I'm not going to let Dad have that kind of power over me. "You can cross that option out."

Luke and Dev exchange glances. Then Luke motions to Dev to go ahead.

"No one's asking you to step down." Dev wipes his brow with a handkerchief. "I'm simply telling you the situation and how things work. The news is all over your dad these days, making it harder to find jury members who haven't heard of him, making your stay longer while the courts can plan a trial. It's a mess none of us want you or Lagan to go through."

"It's like something on the cover of a tabloid," Luke says. "A week ago, the public loved your dad. Now everyone wants to see him hung."

Pulling at his sport coat collar, Dev adds, "Not

everyone. The clerk pulled me aside before I walked in to let me know he's out. Someone just posted his bond."

The words register like a punch in the gut. I wish I could meet the idiot who put up the money to get Dad out of jail. Just so I can thank him... with a punch in his face.

"But that's not our biggest challenge at this moment." Dev brings the conversation back to the charges at hand. "The tough part is that both guys are legally adults now, and if convicted, they face a possible prison term of up to seven years. In your client's case, if the missing item is found, even more."

I slouch and lean back, banging my head against the back of the chair. "And if I had just set the house on fire while Dad slept in his bed one night, I wouldn't be here, facing all this."

"Actually," Dev says, "The fact that the house was never set on fire is the best thing working for you. If it had been, we're looking at double the prison term."

"Is the evidence even any good after all these weeks? I mean, are their actual fingerprints that prove that Lagan or I were in the house?"

"Fingerprint records on the desk drawer where Mr. Vanderbilt's gun was stored, two empty gasoline tins, and a box of matches are the reason you're in here in the first place." Luke shakes his head. "Gotta give it to your dad. Like he prepared for this day."

Maybe it's time I learned something from him. "How can I help? What can I do to give us a fighting chance against my dad? What should I do while I'm waiting?"

"Make a list." Luke and Dev say at the same time, but I hate that word. Luke defers to Dev.

"Yes," Dev says, "Make a list of everyone you know from your childhood forward that might be willing to talk about your character. And your father. Think friends, neighbors, relatives, grandparents, aunts, uncles, cousins, teachers, and coworkers in your dad's case. When I speak with Lagan's parents tonight, this is what I'll be asking them to do as well. And of course Rani, Reggie and Talia will be on Lagan's list."

I swallow, not sure how to tell them. "I'll be honest, there's really no one. We're—we've always been—alone."

"There has to be someone. Everyone has family, even if you don't keep in touch all the time." Luke squinting his eyes like he's trying to think for me.

Try never. I'm shaking my head. Luke closes his computer and files it into his laptop case. Dev does the same with his papers.

"Take some time to think it over." Dev glances at his watch. I know I don't have much time. "Turn over every leaf. Even if you come up with one person, that might be all we need. Someone to say they knew what you and your sister have been going through all these years."

"That would be Mom. She's dead." Talia told Lagan some things, but he was never technically around to witness any of it.

"Or someone who has known how terribly your dad has treated you all these years," Luke says.

"That would be Mom. She's still dead."

"Or someone who knew your dad when he first turned into the person he is today. A parent. A childhood friend. A sibling. A boss?"

Sighing, I feel defeated before entering the ring. Even if I managed to hunt down someone who worked with Dad, who would ever agree to speak up against someone so powerful? No one. "I'll try." What else is there to say?

"Okay, then." Luke gathers his things and shakes my

hand. "I'll see you in the morning." Dev follows suit and the two walk toward the exit.

Not going anywhere. So yes. "I'll see you tomorrow."

13
~Talia~

I guess I should make my way back to the shelter, because Fred's place can't be an option after that staircase encounter. And Lagan's uncle's offer seems sweet, but right now I don't have the energy to meet one more new person.

Walking out of the waiting room, Rani calls my name. "Hey, where ya headed?"

Reggie joins us and says, "Wanna catch a bite to eat with us? My treat, ladies. There's a place around the corner that makes a mean Ginger ale. Light on the ice. Heavy on the ale."

Maybe because I don't know what to do with myself, I swallow my no and follow the two outside to a nearby eatery.

The twenty-four hour diner buzzes with chatter and laughter. The clanking of metal utensils against glass plates grates my senses as the hostess guides us to a booth. Rani and Reggie slide in on one side, and I'm forced to sit across them, like it's two against one. Seconds pass in silence as we all stare at our menus, but I feel Reggie stealing glances at me, like he's trying to read me or something.

Looking up, we meet eye to eye and I blurt out, "What?" He laughs nervously and just shakes his head and then returns to stare at his menu.

"Fine," Rani says. "If he won't say it, I will. You're trouble, and I can't figure out why Lagan is so into you."

So it's my fault that I happen to be the daughter of a lunatic dad. Thanks. I rise to leave and go anywhere but here. Judgment is the last thing I need on a night like tonight. But Reggie follows me and stops me outside the diner doors. The Chicago night air is cool, and the street traffic has died down. Just a few pedestrians tread the sidewalks on both sides of Michigan Ave.

"Don't let Rani get to you," he says, leaning over the railing on the restaurant steps.

The only reason I'm still standing here is I have nowhere to go. I shrug my shoulders, feigning that I don't care.

"But you have to understand where she's coming from," Reggie continues when I don't say anything. "She's like a mama bear, and she, just like you and me, is upset that our boys are in jail. Give her some time, and she'll come around." Reggie pauses long enough for me to look up. Then says, "I, for one, can see exactly why Lagan is into you."

Reggie's smile greets me, pushing back my flight instinct like a gentle wind.

"Umm…" I want to ask what Lagan said about me, but all I can manage is hiding my lips with the back of my hand.

"Lagan's been raving about you and your emerald eyes since day one of college. Sweet to finally see them in person. See you, in person."

Watching a couple pass by on the sidewalk holding hands, the girl leans over and presses a kiss on the guy's cheek, and I long for Lagan something fierce at that moment. Feeling grateful for a friend, I lower my hand, run my thumb over my fingernails and say, "Thank you."

As we walk back in, Reggie leans in, voice lowered: "What did surprise me was that you weren't wearing a long blue gown. I mean, the guy said you wear it everywhere you go, and for a while, I thought maybe you were royalty, and that's why he couldn't bring you around."

Blue gown? The only blue dress I ever wore was on our pretend prom in the middle of the racks at Forever 21. A giggle escapes my lips when I realize that in Lagan's mind, I never took the dress off.

Approaching the table, I rehearse in my head how to respond to Rani if she thrusts another verbal jab at me. I'll act like I didn't hear it. Or I'll find my tough guy voice and say, "Let's take it outside." The very thought of being tough makes me laugh at myself.

A pile of crumpled tissues covers her place mat, and she's blowing her nose when we slide back into the booth. We're all hurting. I don't want to forget that.

"I'm sorry," Rani says after gathering her Kleenex and pushing them off to the side.

"For what?" I ask and she nods.

"Well, I dunno about you ladies, but I am starving!" Reggie looks over his shoulder and the waitress gets the hint and walks over to take our orders.

"What can I get you tonight?" she says, and Rani orders a personal cheese pizza and a Coke. I ask for a Ginger ale.

"And you, sir?"

"I'll take the organic, gluten-free, high-protein, low-carb, fruit salad loaded with antioxidants."

I'm scouring the menu to find what Reggie just

ordered when he lets out a soft chuckle.

"Come again?" she says.

"That's what my buddy Lagan would've ordered, but I'll go with a hamburger, medium to well, no tomatoes, and a side of sweet potato fries. Please."

A smile from Rani affirms Reggie's words, and I get a sudden urge to make a place for Jesse at the table. Scooting to one side of my chair, I do it without saying anything, and I imagine my little brother enjoying the company of new friends too. Friends who like to joke around. Friends who blurt out what they feel, even at the risk of stepping on each other. Friends who go after one another with kindness.

"So how far is your place from here?" Rani asks, and I think back to Jesse's apartment and the less-than-friendly encounter with Fred. "Ow!" Rani says, glaring at Reggie. I felt the brush of his foot that was probably en route to kicking Rani in the leg.

"Maybe she could crash at your place so she won't have to be alone tonight." Reggie's asking Rani, but he's speaking loud enough for me to hear every word.

"Your dad was kind enough to invite me, but I'll be fine," I say, then avert their glances. I don't want to be someone's charity case.

The waitress unloads her tray with the dishes we ordered, placing an ice-cold soda in front of me when Rani's phone buzzes. "Sorry, I have to take this."

As Reggie moves out of the booth to make room for Rani to find a private place to chat, whoever is on the other end of the line speaks so loudly, Rani holds the phone away from her ear as she slides out. And as she walks away, I can hear her—well, the whole restaurant can hear her. "Stop yelling, Mom. This is exactly why Lagan told me not to tell the family."

Placing my cell phone on the tabletop, I pretend not

to notice the drama. I accept that Rani's dad's offer for a bed no longer holds as I scroll the messages aimlessly. Of course there'd be no new messages from either Jesse or Lagan, but I'm tickled to read the last thing Lagan texted Jesse: Tell your sister I'll pick her up in the morn.

Jess's text back reads, K. I'll tell her u cancelled.

Lagan: So yur a funny guy? I'll stop by 2nite & tell her myself.

Jess: She knows. She's been ready since yesterday.

Lagan responded with a wide smiling Emoji. Only thing missing is a dimple.

"Why don't you crash at my place," Reggie says, making me look up from the phone. "I'll take the couch in the lounge. Lagan's bed is empty, and he's a neat freak, so I promise you, it's not like some kind of bachelor pad nightmare."

"But it's a guy's dorm room? Is that even allowed?" And how safe is it? That's what I'm really thinking.

"It's co-ed actually, depending on the suite. So there are a bunch of girls in the suite next to ours. Mostly summer school students like me while Lagan gets to stay as an R.A. Come to think of it, if this whole thing goes south, they might fire him. Man, this just sucks on so many levels." Reggie's hands rub his forehead like he's trying to think of a solution.

"Maybe I should go back to the shelter."

"No way." His eyes meet mine. "Not this time of night. You can go there tomorrow if it's that bad, okay? And I'm sure it'll be fine."

"So it's like an apartment?"

"More like rows of rooms with shared bathrooms, study lounges, and mini-kitchens. But there are locks on the doors, and security watches the entrance twenty-four seven."

Mostly satisfied, I give in. "I left my things back at

Jesse's place." I guess it would be nice to see where Lagan lives. "Maybe we can swing by and pick up my things on the way. Thanks. Really. It means a lot."

"Yeah, are you kidding? Lagan wouldn't have it any other way." Reggie's lips curl down at the edges of his smile, looking kinda Latino with his tan skin and wavy hair on top. What's left of it with that tight haircut, anyway.

Maybe he catches me staring, or maybe he's just really good at distracting me from what's going on, but when I don't say anything, Reggie says, "Go ahead. Guess. I've yet to meet someone who got it right on the first try."

I giggle. I've had the same experience as an ethnic cocktail. "Okay. Half African American, half South Asian."

"Nope. Take two." Reggie has these eyes that almost squint to a close when he smiles really big. Like right now.

"Half black, half Korean?" I ask.

"Closer," Reggie says, mischief dancing in his eyes. "Strike two."

"Okay, half black, half Puerto Rican."

"Sttttr-ike three." Reggie holds up three fingers. "Do we go into overtime, or should I just tell you?"

"Just tell her what?" Rani's back, and she plops down on the booth, making Reggie scoot over. Her expression suggests the phone call did not go well.

"We were just playing that game," Reggie says. "Where you try to put my ethnic puzzle together? Wanna join?"

"Well, Lagan already told me so I'd be cheating." Rani looks over at me. "You guys could be related, actually."

"You're white!" I blurt out. "I mean, half—"

Reggie just laughs. "Mom's half white, half Japanese. And Dad's half black, half Spanish. So you were mostly right."

As Reggie and Rani dig in and start eating, I can't help but ask. "So what do you tell people when they ask?" *Does it ever feel like you don't know where you belong* is what I really want to ask.

Wiping his mouth with his napkin, Reggie takes a sip of ice water. "I'm easy. When I'm on the court playing ball, peeps think I'm black. When friends ask me out to salsa, I put on my best Latino moves. When I'm nerding it out at the computer lab late at night, I'm the Asian guy, and when it's time to cheer on Rick and Darryl while catching up on episodes of *The Walking Dead*, well, I'm just one of the guys. Hey. It works for me."

"*The Walking Dead*?" I've heard of it. Just never thought to watch it. Zombies and blood... yuck.

"Best. Show. Evah!" Rani says.

Silently swirling the ice around with the straw, I wonder if Jesse has a TV in his holding cell.

"How's the soda?" Reggie asks, inhaling the last of his burger. "Stomach feeling a little settled, yet?"

"You know he's pre-med, right?" Rani adds. "Don't let him turn you into his patient."

"So I should sleep with one eye open? In case you try and stick me with a needle in the middle of the night." I can joke. A little.

Reggie smiles. "Talia can lock the dorm room door. We're good."

"Thanks," Rani says softly, and I recognize that look of relief in her eyes. Reggie saved her from something I've dealt with my whole life—having to explain her family.

When the waitress brings the bill, I pull out a couple of singles from my bag, thankful Jesse gave me money, but Reggie gives the waitress a card and says, "I got this."

Thanks, I say with a smile.

"Thanks, Reg," Rani says, "I'll get it next time. Text me your Starbucks orders in the morning."

"Happy to whip up some eggs for you two, if you like?" Reggie says.

"Sure." I should be able to eat again by the morning. I look down at the phone. Of course, Rani and Reggie's names are saved in Lagan's contacts. As we walk out into the night, I can't find my name.

"Look under favorites," Rani says, glancing over my shoulder.

Sure enough. There it is, the only name under Favorites. I smile as I read Lagan's entry. No number. No contact info. Just my name: Talia Grace. Aka Dewdrop.

14
~Jesse~

Nothing will happen till the morning, giving me less than twelve hours to think of all the jobs I can work at when I get out of here. Ways I can save up lots of money with one purchase in mind. To hire a hit man to kill Dad once and for all. Or in the very least handcuff him to an airplane and transport him to his native South Africa. Out of sight...

"Light's out," someone says on the speaker overhead. I scarf down the sandwich the officer left me and finish off a water bottle, and lay back on the cot, allowing my eyes to adjust to the darkness. The barred door is locked and I can hear muttering from the guy in the adjacent cell. Everyone has a mantra. His seems to be, "One more night. Just one more night." The somber tone of his voice makes me wonder how many nights he's been repeating it.

I don't know when my neighbor's voice faded and I fell asleep. I do know that the night pushed me back in time. Back to a place when I was four, and it was the morning of Talia's sixth birthday.

"Now you go to school, work your hardest, and

make us proud, okay?" Dad said to Talia at the breakfast table.

"Even on her birthday?" I answered. "Can't she just play since it's her birthday?"

Dad moved behind me and put his hands on my shoulders, giving them an uncomfortably tight squeeze. "Playing leads to disaster, Justice. We Vanderbilts pride ourselves on never taking a day off." With another pinching squeeze, Dad looked me square in the eye, then took his workbag and travel coffee mug and headed out the door. No happy birthday. No kiss on Talia's forehead. No presents.

Mom watched Dad through the kitchen window until he drove off, hung her apron hurriedly over a wall hook and then ushered us into the double stroller.

"Mommy, I'm six," Talia said. "I'm too big for this now."

"Won't we be late to school if you take us, Mommy?" I asked. "I'll take the bus. Talia can have a special ride from you."

But Mom ignored me and guided me into the front of the stroller and buckled me in, shifting the belt to the back where I couldn't reach it.

"Mommy, my backpack!" Talia squealed as we exited the house on that spring morning. Come to think of it, she had forgotten mine too. But Mom ignored us both and began pushing us down the sidewalk in the opposite direction of school.

After a few minutes of uncomfortable silence, Talia started giggling. I turned to face her. "What? What's so funny?"

"Don't you see?" she whispered, but I'm sure Mom could hear her. "Mom's surprising me for my birthday!"

"We're going to get cake?" I asked, but I was four. I had no idea which way the bakery was. I simply loved the idea of cake for breakfast.

"Not cake, stupid."

"Apologize, Talia." Mom's voice was stern. "We don't call each other names."

"So-rry," Talia said, "But Mom! He's so dumb, he doesn't realize that you're making my birthday wish come true! A day off!"

Mom resumed silently pushing us down side streets, turning this way and that, and when we reached the outer edge of the sandy beaches of Benton Harbor, I whimpered. "So... no cake?"

"Something better than cake," Mom said, but she kept her eyes straight ahead, like she saw a finish line where all I saw was sand and the water's edge on an empty beach. And like a racecar driver cutting off a motorcycle, my memories skid to a stop as I wake up with sweat on my brow.

Unable to fall back asleep, I resort to making the thing I despise most just to pass the aching minutes of the night. A list. Of all the things I'll do to make this all right when I get out of here. I'll find Talia and me a new place. I'll work extra hours with Jimmy to make the money for all these friggin' lawyer fees that I'm sure are adding up. I'll talk to Summer. And I'll... I haven't figured out what I'll say to her.

It's bad enough we started out with me lying to her about my name. Maybe I need to give her some space rather than drag her into this mess. And I'll figure out how to get to Texas. What I need to do to enroll in the Air Force. And I'll do it alone. I've spent enough time depending on people for help. It's time I grow up and be the man in the family. It's my turn to step up. Get in the ring. And give Dad the fight of his life. And there won't be anything pretty about Dad going down.

15
~Talia~

Rani catches a cab before I tell Reggie I never got the key to Jesse's hostel, and one in the morning is not the time to go knocking on Fred's door.

"No problem," Reggie says. "There's a Rite Aid near the dorms. You can pick up a toothbrush. And I'm sure Lagan won't mind if you borrow a t-shirt to sleep in and stuff. Just get your things in the morning."

I agree, liking Lagan's roommate more with every passing minute. Taking the El back a few stops, we walk up five flights to his dorm room. Passing a few guys who greet Reggie, they give me a once-over, and then look back at Reg.

"She's my little sister," he says. "And. She's taken." The guys move aside and keep moving.

When Reggie unlocks the door, I say, "Thanks. I never had a big brother."

"And I'm an only child, so can you imagine the treat it is for me, baby sis?" Reggie pushes the door open and flips the light switch. "Home sweet home."

Standing in the doorway, the side of the room belonging to Lagan has to be on the left. The Post-its on his desk and Bulls posters under his loft bed confirm my suspicions. Reggie's side of the room is just as neatly kept as Lagan's. I spot a crate flipped on its side as a make shift pantry shelf, a poster of *The Walking Dead* with a cop pointing a gun, and another with a soccer player, jumping off the field. Reggie's bed is lofted too, and desks and black and grey beanbag chairs grace each corner. A guitar lies outside its case against the beanbag on Lagan's side. Makes me wonder what song he was strumming when the cops knocked on his door.

"Not bad for a guy's dorm, right?" Reggie says, grabbing a pillow and blanket off his bed, sheets from a dresser drawer and some clothes and his toothbrush. "It's all yours. Feel free to lock it at night, and the girls' bathrooms are down the hallway past the swinging doors that separate the suites. We passed one on the way, remember?"

"Thanks again, Reggie." Starting to feel bad for kicking him out, I say, "I could take the lounge—"

"So now you want to fight me for the couch? Nope." Reggie's outside the door now, peering around the corner. "Plus the TV is out here and unless you want to lose sleep to the guy who always strolls in around three in the morning and can't go to bed without watching CNN, I'll be right over here if you need anything, okay? And of course, feel free to help yourself to whatever you need."

Reggie disappears and I shut the door and turn the bolt to lock. Alone with Lagan's stuff, I'm tempted to go through all his things. Who am I kidding? It would just be too easy to snoop around, but I'd rather he show me himself as he's ready.

After finding a phone charger, I slip into a Bulls t-shirt from his top drawer, turn off the lights and climb up the loft bed, pulling the comforter over me. So this is where you lie every night and dream about me?

When I settle onto my back, I'm tickled by what I see on the ceiling. The letters T and L made of Post-its. A single yellow Post-it hangs between them. I sit up to read what's printed on it. It's our word. The promise we made to each other. To wait. Even if it takes…

Forevah.

16
~Talia~

As I close my eyes to sleep in Lagan's bed, I leave this world long enough to meet an old friend—the woman in the garden. She followed the gardener and a tiny touch of his back stopped her bleeding. She wants me to follow her. She's one step behind the gardener, the crowds dispersed, watching him plant seeds. But the seeds are different. Shiny. Like diamonds. He takes them one by one from the pocket over his chest. And as he puts them in place, I realize his earth is black. And the seeds...they're stars.

Awake now, I carefully descend the loft steps to the ground and pull back the curtains, no stars in sight but one. The North Star still lingers while the colors of a new day peel across the sky over Lake Michigan, and the alarm clock on Lagan's desk reads 6:14AM. Rather than bothering Reggie, I write him a quick note on a Sticky to tell him I'll be back soon, and pull on my sneakers after changing back into yesterday's clothes.

When I exit the dorms, I size up the distance to the water and back to Jesse's apartment, estimating the round trip job could take me an hour if all goes smoothly. All, meaning my inevitable face to face with Fred if I want my things back. Reaching for my neck I find the chain and trace it till my fingers hold the heart. *Please, let them be okay.*

I start my jog by heading two blocks east to the lake. The rising sun shimmering on the water makes Lake Michigan look like a sea of diamonds. Orienting myself, I backtrack toward the Red line on the El and run under the tracks for several stops. Stopping to catch my breath, the scent of freshly baked bagels fills my senses. Wanting to save my appetite for Reggie's eggs, I pop into the nearest deli and settle for a mini onion bagel with cream cheese, walking the last few blocks.

Fred's nowhere in sight when I make it up the two flights to Jesse's floor, but the smell of wet paint fills the air. Two garbage bags line the hallway, and Jesse's door is wide open. The room, freshly painted, looks bare of any sign of life. I get it. We've been kicked out. I find Jesse's and my things in the black bags, confirming my suspicion. As I carry the bags to the ground floor, the debate to beg Fred for a second chance dissipates with the awareness that I don't know where Fred is.

While keeping an eye out to hail a cab, I check the phone to see if anyone's tried to contact me. There are three missed texts, one from Reggie and the other two from Rani. She couldn't sleep so she came over early.

Breakfast's ready & a hot chai tea latte is waitin 4 U. Hope it was okay that I ordered for you. You didn't respond to my 1st text. Where R U?

I text back: On my way.

Reggie's reads: Eggs are getting cold.

I retype the same text I just sent Rani and hit send.

Two cabs pull around the corner, the first already taken, but the second one stops, and the driver loads my bags in the trunk. "Laundry day?" he says, with a strong accent I can't identify.

"Something like that. Superior and Lake Shore Drive please. Northwestern's campus."

Mr. Cab Driver gets the hint and turns his music up while I watch morning commuters hustle and bustle, many carrying coffee cups while staring at phones.

Between the jog and lugging the bags up six flights of stairs, I can check off morning workout. Before I push through the suite doors, I can hear Rani's voice. "Should we tell her now or later?"

"Now," I say, heaving the bags on the floor in front of them. "Are Jesse and Lagan okay?"

Reggie motions to a seat at the table where the plates and utensils lie untouched.

"Just tell me," I say. The eggs can wait.

My phone buzzes in my pocket before Rani can answer. Luke, texting me: Everything's gonna be okay. The bail hearing is over. Good news: Case dropped.

I text back, Wow! Okay.

"I got the news!" I say, happy enough to do a cartwheel. If I could. I can't.

"I'm gonna nuke your latte." Rani busies herself in the mini kitchen on the far wall.

Reggie takes my bags inside his room and returns to the lounge. I'm still standing where he left me. "If you need towels or anything to wash up. Or if you're hungry, eat first. Whatever you need…"

"Reggie." I stop him.

He's trying. He really is. I just need a moment to take it in. The case is dropped. Jesse and Lagan should be released. How long does all that take? I walk over to the windows where the brilliance of the morning sun washes out the waves on the water, making the lake look still and peaceful, a glass top that stretches to the horizon.

"So the eggs," I turn to join my two new friends.

"Who taught you to cook?"

"My dad," Reggie says. "Mom can't cook to save her life. Grandma tried to teach her how to perfect a cobbler, but she was more interested in fixing cars and racing them. That's how she met my dad, so I guess it all worked out." Reggie scoops me some eggs, prettied up with tiny green and red peppers.

"Dad on the other hand learned how to cook on a Navy ship. He was the head chef, and he wanted the Seals to eat good so he practiced and taste-tested all his meals before he agreed to serve them." Reggie pats his flat stomach, "Needless to say, Dad paid for all that tasting over the years. He has a belly that's more like a six pack of jelly donuts."

Rani laughs. I join in. And then dig into the eggs. "Yum," I say. Because they are, and Reggie smiles, pleased with himself.

Even as it seems like the minutes are crawling by, all three of our phones begin to buzz. Texts coming in. Mine is from Lagan. I look up, and both Reggie and Rani's faces beam.

"Let's go!" Rani says, and we head down the stairs and just as we exit the brick building, a cab pulls up and Jesse and Lagan emerge from opened car doors.

"The case got dropped," Jesse says. "I have no idea how."

I look at Lagan, a smile on his face, but he's shaking his head. "All we know is that our lawyers rock! They somehow convinced the judge that the evidence had holes in it, and he agreed, banged his gavel and said, 'Case dismissed.'"

"That's crae!" Reggie says.

"As in crazy-awesome!" Rani gives Lagan a high five.

At this moment, I could care less how or why it happened. My shoulders sandwiched between my two favorite guys, I'm just thrilled they're here.

17
~Talia~

While Reggie and Rani prep another round of eggs, the rest of us shower up for the day. Jesse is happy to find his clothes in the black bags. Not so happy to hear we were officially kicked out of Fred's place.

When we're all seated around the lounge to eat, the questions begin to fly.

Rani goes first. "Soooo… What's it like to be in jail?"

"And the food? Do they really serve it on metal trays, and does everything look and taste like boxed mashed potatoes?" Reggie asks.

"Did they take your mug shot?" Rani throws in. "And did some guy named Vinnie ask you for some smokes?"

Can't say I didn't want to know either. I turn my attention to Jesse who chews his food slowly, having just pulled off a bite of eggs.

Lagan shoots Jesse a look and shrugs his shoulders. "No one offered me mashed potatoes. I had a sandwich last night. Bologna I think. Which made me decide—if I ever go back—to make sure to tell them I'm allergic. To Bologna and boxed mashed potatoes. And smoking."

Everyone laughs. Everyone except Jesse. When the noise dies down, all eyes turn to my brother.

"Close your eyes," Jesse says, putting his fork down on his plate. I look around and see everyone obey so I do too. Then I hear Jesse say, "That's what prison is like.

"Dark?" Rani asks.

"Blinding?" Reggie throws in his own word.

But I know what word Jesse's getting at, because I know my brother. *Hopeless.*

One by one, we open our eyes, and I push the eggs around the plate with my fork.

After several minutes of awkward silence, Lagan rises to clear plates. "We should celebrate. A round of Starbucks on me! What do you guys say?"

"I have somewhere to go," Jesse says, and our eyes meet. "Okay, someone to see and some things to take care of," he adds.

"And I need to get my old job back." I'm thinking of the funds we'll need to get a new place as I finish cleaning up with Lagan.

Reggie disappears into his room and emerges with his backpack. "Anyone want to hit the library with me?"

Lagan glances from me to Reggie then back to me. "Kinda have to show my face at my parents and make peace. I think it's time they meet Talia too."

Is he asking? Because that sounded more like an announcement.

Jesse motions to follow him into the bedroom. "Can I talk to you for a sec?" My feet move toward my brother, but my mind stays with what Lagan just said.

Once alone, Jesse reaches into one bag, pulls out a pair of long white sport socks, tied together but rigid in their shape. Pulling out some bills from inside one sock, he says, "Here. And if you need any more, just take it."

I peek inside the socks as he shoves bills back in. "What? Where did you get all this money?" Suddenly I'm afraid he stole it. "What if the cops had noticed?"

"It's not against the law to make your sock drawer your bank account," Jesse says. "Anyway. I worked for it. Every last dollar. We're gonna be all right. I'll talk to Jimmy today. He might have a job for me."

"What about a place?" I glance up at Lagan's bed, doubting that's an option tonight.

"I'm on it." Jess ties up the socks and shoves them deep into the garbage bag. "Trust me, Jimmy's cool. I should know something by tonight."

I hand Jesse the phone he gave me. "Keep me posted. I'll be with Lagan so you can text him if you find out something sooner." I hug my brother tightly.

"What?" Jesse backs away and waits for me to meet his gaze.

"It's just…" I hate admitting it. "Be careful. He's out there. And…I'm scared."

"We've been through worse. And you'll be with Lagan, right?"

I know he's right. "I'll see you soon." SUS, as Lagan would say.

Jesse heads out and soon after Lagan knocks on the open door. "You all right?"

"You're funny. This is your room. You don't have to knock to come in."

Lagan's eyesight roams up his loft. "Heard someone's been sleeping in my bed. Should I start calling you, Goldi, Dewdrop?"

"You're not gonna call me Dewdrop in front of your parents, are you?" I ask, pushing him playfully in the chest. "Talia works just fine."

"Okay, Dewdrop." Lagan smiles, his dimple a lighthouse to my ship sailing off course. "Only when

67

we're alone."

I grab my blue satchel and move past him to the doorway. Taking a deep breath, I say the name I've been calling Lagan in my head. "Coming, Prince?"

Lagan laughs out loud, throws a baseball hat on, and swoops me up off my feet from behind till we're out of his dorm room. "Oh. Sorry. Thought I saw a dragon."

Reggie and Rani laugh. I push his hands off my waist and shake my head.

"Thanks for the eggs, man," Lagan says, chest bumping Reggie, and then he tousles Rani's hair. "See ya later, Cuz. And don't distract my boy. He's gotta get straight A's if he's gonna get into med school."

"Distract? Pu-lease," Rani says. "I'm going thrift-shop hunting for apartment furniture. And good luck with the parents."

Lagan takes my hand in his, and talks to them while locking eyes with me. "Oh, I'm sure they'll love her."

Then silently, I read his lips as he mouths the words, "Cuz, I love you," and we head across the hall, down the stairs, and into a new day.

18
~Talia~

Walking hand in hand up Huron Street, if I close my mind to all that lies behind and all that could happen tomorrow, I find that place in between I never thought existed. This place called now. Lagan. He's with me, for now, and I wouldn't want to be any other place.

His fingers shift and his thumb slides over my palm and every cell in my hand tingles. Aware. I'm so aware you're here. I'm here. Together.

Almost at the El, Lagan agrees when I say, "It's okay to stop by the garden first?" I'm not sure what I'm more nervous about—meeting Lagan's parents or seeing the fire damage to the garden. Letting go of Lagan's hand and rubbing my arms over my green sleeves, a shudder replaces my moment of now. I know full well that nothing and no one ever fully recovers from being burned.

"I'm here, okay," Lagan says, reminding me once again why I adore him. He doesn't ask what's wrong. He doesn't offer to fix me. He just wants me to know I'm not alone. And that's exactly what I need after getting off the Metra at the Train Station, and we trek the

69

distance to the garden entrance.

Seeing the caution tape draped across the barriers, we cross the nearly empty parking lot and spot a sign that reads, "Under Reconstruction". Lagan waits patiently for me as I stand cemented to the sidewalk at the gate's entrance, taking in the dingy white ash blanketing my view where once shades of green filled nearly every corner.

Several deep breaths later, the sound of voices ahead awakens my motivation to move forward. Maybe that's Jason, the sweet friend who taught me all things gardening. Or the boss, and he's looking for help to get this place back in order.

Walking around the charred gate, Lagan follows and I head to where the Park Office used to be, but it's all boarded up, the windows totally missing. Following the broken up trail toward the willow tree, I spot two guys working at the soil, carrying bags behind them as they move from spot to spot.

"Hey," I call out, and they turn to listen. "Is Jason around?"

They motion up the pathway and resume working. Lagan and I pass them, knowing the willow is not much further from this spot.

"Sorry, no trespassing while all the work is being done. There's still a lot of falling branches and damage that make the garden dangerous for the public."

"We won't be long," Lagan says. "Talia used to work here. She just wants to see the place she used to work."

"Where exactly did you work?" The first guy's coworker approaches and joins the conversation, their white overalls filthy grey like coal miners' might look after coming up from the caves.

I clear my throat and say, "The water—I mean, weeping willow. At the back of the big field." I'm saying the words, but they're both looking at me like they've never heard of it.

Then one slaps the other in the arm. "I know which one she's talking about. You must be Talia." The first guy says, "Jason's mentioned you. He's been working overtime trying to get this place back in shape." He stops and does a one-eighty with his neck. "As you can see, it's gonna be a while."

"Were you here the night of the fire?" Lagan asks.

The two exchange glances, as the taller of the two digs his spade into the ground to make it stand on its own.

"Name's Nate and this here's Sergio. You might want to ask Jason about that."

Finding Jason up by the shed, or where the shed of tools used to be, I make to run up to him, but Lagan grabs my arm, keeping me from tripping over fallen debris.

Jason sees us coming and meets us half way, the pathway the only sort of safe place to tread. "Hey."

"Hey yourself." And Jason steps back from my motion to hug him. "Don't want to mess up your clothes." He's just as covered with dirt as Sergio and Nate. Maybe more. "I wouldn't go back there if I were you."

Jason knows why I came.

"How bad was it?" I ask, but the answer lies all around me. "When can I start working again? It's obvious you guys can use the help."

Lagan adds, "And I don't mind throwing in a few hours here and there too. Just as a volunteer."

Jason doesn't answer right away. Letting out a huge sigh, he apologizes first. Then explains. "That night, the fire spread fast, and it didn't help that we hadn't had rain in weeks. But then out of the blue, thunder pounds and a summer storm takes full effect. Which in theory should have been great. The firefighters were just arriving and the rain helped put out some of the smaller fires. So we all headed out to the lot. But the storm made it harder for the firefighters to work, and the boss was in his element when the cops arrived, interrogating each of us about who had visited that evening. Any suspicious activity we'd noticed and failed to report. Anyone who walked through here that night looking for trouble whom we'd dismissed." Jason pauses and looks me right in the eyes. "Talia. I already told you your dad came by that night. I had to tell the boss. And...it's a miracle he didn't fire me too."

Before he says the words I already know. There's no way I'm getting my job back. I turn away from Jason and Lagan and just stare at the damage all around me. *Sheesh, Dad, you can't leave even one thing in my life alone.*

Lagan breaks the echoing silence first. "If we're really careful, can we just swing by and see the tree?"

"Do what you want, but if the boss sees you back there, he's not gonna be happy. And Talia," Jason puts one hand on my arm. "I tried to tell him you weren't even around the night of the fire, but he wouldn't buy it. Especially since you didn't come back. Sorry."

Silently we push forward down the trail to where the green lawn used to be. Each passing step is like walking through a wasteland. There are downed trees, charred branches, and little sign of life. When we reach the clearing, the great lawn that I walked over many days is just a field of dirt, with patches of straw-like stubble.

"There she is," Lagan says.

"Was." She's gone. Her majesty dwindled down to a trashed umbrella. A few branches pierce the air like a child's first pencil drawing of a tree.

I start to walk toward her, our once waterfall willow,

but Lagan snags my arm again. "I think maybe this is close enough. For today."

I know he's right, but I just want to be closer. Feel her last branches. Touch her broken trunk. Say goodbye.

Lagan knows me, and he knows I need to do what I need to do. Her missing leaves and withered branches make her look aged and naked. I tread the field carefully till the willow is inches from me.

"I'm sorry," I whisper to my friend, the one who gave me shade, comfort, and a place to discover myself. "I'm sorry," I sputter the words again, reaching to touch her branches that crumble in my hands, ashes left on my palm. Backing away, I take one last look, fighting back tears, and say the words I came here to say: "Thank you."

19
~Talia~

"Dewdrop for your thoughts," Lagan says when we're back at the train station waiting for the Metra. The nickname's growing on me, but I don't see the point of answering.

After what Dad tried to pull with the arrest and seeing the garden all destroyed, I know he'll stop at nothing to steal everything and everyone that's important to me. How do I live like this?

The sound of the oncoming train muffles the question in the air, and when we board and sit down, I lean my head on Lagan's shoulder and stare out the window, wondering how my little brother's day is going. It's completely blue skies save a scattering cloud here and there. There was a time when Lagan fought so hard to swim through my clouds to know me. Now I struggle to know how to tell him that the clouds might never leave. And...

Lagan presses a Sticky on my jeans, and I can feel his eyes on me, waiting for me to read it.

The note reads: Do you know your ABC's?

He wants a dewdrop, even if I can only write it

down.

I take the pen and Post-its and think of what I want him to know no matter what happens with Dad.

A is 4 Always. Always and forever is about how long I want to be with you.

Out of the corner of my eye, I see a dimple reappear slowly. Then he playfully snags the pen and pad from my fingers and writes me back.

B is 4 Brave. You were Brave today to face the willow. Oh & Beautiful. Always.

Then I write,

C is 4 Cute. Yur Cute. I don't feel Brave when I think of my dad. But yur Always Cute.

And he raises his eyebrows playfully as he writes back,

D is 4 Dance. Be Brave & Dance with me. Cuz yur Always Cute even tho u can't Dance.

Punching his shoulder playfully, I regain my balance, aware that we have to transfer trains at the next stop. Just enough time for one more Post-it. It's time I tell him what I was thinking when we first got on the train.

E is 4 Edge. I feel like I'm living on the Edge.

Lagan scrawls a Post-it in record time and I barely read the words—F is 4 us. 4-evah! Forever—when he says, "Let's go!" and we race off the train just as the last ding sounds the closing doors.

"Just trying to help you live on the edge," Lagan says. "Dance with me?"

He doesn't get it. I don't want to live on the edge, but he's such a nut, and that dimple. Selfishly not wanting it to disappear, I focus on the Post-its. "And chance you showing up at your parents with broken toes? It's gonna be hard enough to win them over when they find out it's my dad who tried to put you in jail." Failed attempt 101 to keep Dad out of my thoughts.

Ugh.

"They'll love you." Lagan pulls me in closer to his side as we walk toward a bench and sit down. Then he turns my face so I can't avoid his eyes.

How could I forget the sound of Rani's mother through the phone? "If you say so, but Rani said they are pretty upset."

"At me." Lagan finishes my sentence. "And they should be. I'm trying to be an adult and not bother them about every little thing that goes wrong…"

"Umm…jail isn't such a little thing." His parents might not buy that argument.

"You have a point, but I'm not a convicted criminal. I figured the arrest would blow over once my uncle got there. And luckily it did."

"Are you changing your mind? Do you think we should just let it go?" L.I.G. That was another one of Lagan's acronyms we once said to each other when we agreed to let each other go so I could find temporary safety at the shelter.

The sound of the railroad gate coming down over the track reverberates. Our train is almost here. Lagan runs his hand over my hair and down my cheek, letting two fingers rest there. "The only thing I want you to let go of is any thought of backing down. But I have to admit, it's gonna be a fight. A lot harder one than I imagined."

I look down the tracks, trying to remember how far we've come. The tracks on the other side remind me we have so much further to go.

Lagan wraps his hands around mine. He'll be my boxing gloves. "A perfect fit, if you ask me."

SOARING THROUGH STARS

20
~Jesse~

Jumping on the Red Line, I get off a few blocks from
Jimmy's mom's place. I stop by Fred's to pick up my
deposit. Just guessing that this whole trial nonsense is
going to cost an arm and a leg, money is up there on my
priority list. Right next to a bed to sleep in tonight.

Smoke rises from the ashtray on Fred's desk, but the
landlord is not behind his desk. The sound of a toilet
flushing from nearby stops me from exiting, and Fred
emerges from the restroom, zipping up his jeans.

"Back so soon? Did you break out?" Fred says,
picking up his half-used cigarette and taking a long drag.

"Just wanted to thank you for letting me stay here
and pick up my deposit."

"Deposit?" Fred's jovial tone turns sour. "As in the
money I owed you if you hadn't left all your crap in my
place. Or if I didn't have to pack up your stuff. Or if I
didn't have to clean up your mess. How 'bout I sue you
for bringing cops in this place and making the neighbors
think I'm housing drug dealers? Who's gonna wanna
rent the room now?"

Fred's still going on when I turn and leave his office.

The last thing I hear are how many thousands I've cost him for taking a chance on me. How he's sorry he took a chance on me. I'm starting to wonder if he's right.

I don't technically know where Jimmy lives, only that the last few times he hired me, we put together a new fence around his mom's yard. Dad never taught me anything about tools so it's been fun too, learning to build and fix things at the different properties, but the best part's been just having a guy to talk to.

Spotting the white painted fence ahead, I smile to myself as I think about how Jimmy knew I had a crush on Summer before I ever told him her name, and as upset as I am about Fred kicking me and my sister out of the apartment, I guess I still have to thank him for introducing me to Jimmy.

Pushing the gate open, I'm tempted to walk around back and see if roses still bloom in Amanda's garden. Jimmy's mom helped me put together my first flowers that I ever gave to a girl. Summer loved them too, and just thinking about her strengthens my resolve to get my life together and give Dad the fight of his life. I knock a few times and wait, no one answers, and just when I've given up, I turn and see Jimmy coming up the walkway, carrying what looks like groceries in his arms.

"Well, well. Look who came back from the grave?" Jimmy puts the brown paper bags down on the porch and shakes my hand. "Dude, I almost went hunting for that girl you said you liked, wondering if she was bad news. And then you call me one time to tell me you're in the hospital. Then I don't hear from you. Are you better? Everything cool now?"

"I was just… I had a little situation," I say, fumbling for words, suddenly nervous that Fred's already mentioned the cops to him.

"Go on." Jimmy unlocks the front door and opens it

for me to enter.

I pick up one of the bags and carry it in, saying, "The hospital thing lasted a few weeks, but I'm better now. Much better." I don't add that my side still aches a bit and I leave out the part about my dad trying to put me in jail for life.

"Great. Ready to work again?"

But before I can answer, Amanda meets us and says, "Jimmy, you put the groceries away while I fix you two hard-working gentlemen some lemonade."

I'm looking around, not sure if I should follow, or sit, or help with the groceries.

"Hand me the milk, will ya?" Jimmy says, and I do, and together we empty the bags of fruit and veggies. Bread and eggs. Frozen pizza and ice cream.

"Sit, sit," Amanda says, and the three of us take seats at the kitchen table. "How you been, Jesse? You never came back to tell me if she liked the flowers?"

"She loved them."

"Ma, your memory's flipping out on you again." Jimmy's looking at her funny. "His name's John. And leave John alone. I'm sure he'll figure out the girl thing on his own."

"A little help from a lady who's been around the block a few times isn't a bad thing."

Exchanging smiles with Amanda, I also feel stupid. I never told Jimmy my real name, and now I have to confess. "The name's actually Jesse. I just... well, never liked my name." Tasting the lemonade, I add, "But the reason I stopped by today was to see if you had any jobs lined up that I could help you with right away?"

"Wanna babysit Mom?" Jimmy says, and Amanda nudges Jimmy like she means to push him off his chair.

"I don't need anyone to watch me, Jimmy, although I do enjoy Jesse's company." She smiles at me, refilling all our glasses with more lemonade.

"Ma, come on. Last week, you left the teakettle on a lit burner and went for your morning walk. And yesterday, you slept all night with the windows open and the temperature dropped to the forties."

"I suppose a little reminder or two couldn't hurt, but I'm just not understanding all this technology the young people use these days. Text messages and that iPad you bought me. I still can't figure out how to turn it off, and it keeps changing the password on me."

I notice the tablet sitting on the kitchen counter, closed, several cook books piled on top of it. "I could show you a few things if you like," I offer, wondering if they really do need someone to live here and help. "If it helps, I could stick around too. I was…umm…looking for a new place to stay, actually."

"If he's gonna help you, shouldn't you at least feed him and give him a roof over his head?" Jimmy eyes me, maybe gauging if I'm seriously open to it.

"I could stay." I slow down. "I mean, if it's helpful. And I'd pay rent too. I would never expect to stay for free. And I'd stay out of your way, but if you needed help, I'd help." Sounding like Summer with her gift of chatter, I force myself to step back. And wait.

"But can you cook?" Amanda asks. "Because as much as I've loved cooking all these years, I wouldn't mind a meal made once in a while."

I swallow, chewing on my words before I say them. "I don't really know how, but I have a sister. She learned how to cook really well after our mom, umm, passed away. But we're doing fine now. Really we are."

"Jimmy, whaddya waiting for? Go make the guest rooms up for Jesse and his sister. Is today too soon? And don't worry, we'll work out the rent and all that. First things first, if my son wants me to have someone around, at least I get some say in who I keep around. And I'm pretty sure your sister and I will get along. What's her name?"

"Talia. Talia Grace Vanderbilt." Checking my cell, I notice a few missed texts from Lagan. "Sorry, she's been worried about me. Let me just tell her I'm okay. And I found a place for us." I let the last line slip, but Jimmy rises to check the rooms, and Amanda just nods. No one's making a big deal out of it. And I keep my eyes lowered on the phone screen as I try to contain my wonder at it all.

I text Lagan: Tell my sister found a place for us.

Amanda puts the lemonade jar back and files the glasses into the dishwasher.

"Let me help you with those."

She resists. "You get to stay if you don't treat me like an ol' lady. And I'll ask you for help when I need it. Is that good?"

I nod, yes. She sounds a lot like me when I was rehabbing my legs. I wanted to fight my way back, alone. But I needed Talia's help at times, and now when I look back on that last couple of years, I think the hardest part might have been for Talia to watch me and refrain from helping me every chance she had.

Heading to the front door, I say, "If it's okay, I'll be by later with my things. And I'll bring Talia to meet you. Should I call you when I'm on my way?"

Jimmy comes back down the stairs and meets us at the entrance. "Just call me. Mom can't find her cell phone half the time. And if you're free, I have a job I could use your help on this next weekend. It's a big job but it also pays, so just let me know."

I say, yes, right away and "Thanks," and head out the door back to the train. Silently thanking my lucky stars, I climb the steps up to the El, jump on the Red Line, and watch the doors shut.

The train barely begins to roll down the tracks when my phone rings. It's Jimmy.

"Just spoke with Fred. Says you've had a run-in with the cops." Jimmy keeps talking without giving me a chance to explain. "Man, I am so sorry, but whatever the story is, I can't exactly let someone in trouble with the law stay in the same house with my mom. I'm really sorry, but I'm sure you understand."

"But the charges were dropped."

"Arson's no small matter, my friend."

I don't think he heard me.

"Fred says a couple of guys, one a hot shot lawyer, were snooping around looking for a gun. Dude, you lied to me about your name, too. Whatever, she's my mom. Gotta think of her safety. You understand, right?"

We sit on the phone while silence passes between us. I have nothing to say. I failed to keep my own mom safe, so yeah, I get it. I got nothing.

"About the job next week?" I ask, hating the desperation I hear in my own voice.

"Yeah, don't worry 'bout it. I got a guy who said he'd help me out. I'm good."

That makes one of us.

Jimmy waits another beat before signing off. "Okay, then. Gotta run. Mom's calling."

And so is mine—from the grave. Reminding me I can't depend on anybody.

21
~Jesse~

Entering the library downtown, I fiddle with the zipper on my backpack, wondering if there's a how-to book on ten ways to screw up your life. Oh wait, I could write that book in one line: be the son of Gerard Vanderbilt.

Reminding myself I have a good reason to see her— those churros aren't going to pay themselves back on their own—a dull pain from the right side of my back nudges me like a push off a cliff.

The glass dome above the library foyer reveals blue and sun, not a cloud in the sky. Funny how if it hadn't been raining that night, I might have never met Summer and her sisters outside the garden where Talia was supposed to be. Summer would have never offered me her blue poncho. I'd have never had to return it and then ruin it in the washing machine. I know she said one churro date at a time, but maybe if I buy her a bunch, I can back away from this day with one strand of dignity.

She's sitting at the same cubicle where I first spotted her that day in the library when I came to email Dad. Like the sun brushed its fingertips over her pretty head, the blond highlights seem more pronounced on the bottom half of her brown hair that falls just past her shoulders over her light green sweater. Her sleeve covers a vine of leaves tattoo on her upper arm. I'm betting she's wearing a skirt. Her legs are under the table, but her mind's elsewhere as she stares out the library window. Wonder if she's thinking of me?

Peeking over her cubicle, I toss the words I rehearsed this morning—Excuse me, Miss, but is this a good time to take a churro study break?—swallow a thousand apologies, and simply say, "Hey."

Looking up from her book, smile beaming, Summer says, "John!" a little loudly for the taste of nearby patrons who shush her immediately. "Sorry, still getting used to Jesse. But wait, that means more churros, right?"

As she follows me to the exit, I was right about the skirt. She's wearing a pink one. My head spins the moment she takes my hand in hers, and as I squeeze in behind her in the limited space of the revolving door, I'm acutely aware of how close our bodies are. What did I come here to tell her, again?

"No more wheelchair?" Summer asks before we get outside. "Does that mean you're better? When did you get out? I know it's only been a few days, but are you back home? How's your sister?"

I'm dizzy with all her questions, but I just want her to keep talking as we walk over to the park, lured by the scent of hot, cinnamon-gardener churros.

"Are you going to Texas? Did you find out about the Air Force? Will they give you a hard time about not knowing how to swim? Maybe you should learn to swim before you go?" And with that last question, Summer lets go of my hand and throws her arms around my neck. "I am just thrilled to see you."

Really? Because, I couldn't tell. Stepping to the left to let pedestrians pass, I move Summer with me, and then guide her to turn facing forward again. "So, do you still like the ones filled with chocolate?" Chicago streets are not conducive to walking backward. Not at this time of the day, anyway.

Hand holding mine again, Summer says, "Yes. Anything. I'm really glad you're here. I was just daydreaming about…"

Me?

"Churros." Summer rubs her tummy with her free hand. "And eating churros with you beats eating them alone."

I order three dozen and she gives me a nudge in the side, making me turn so she won't see me wince with pain. "He means three."

"John, right?" The Churro Guy eyes me curiously as I take extra napkins and slide over bills. "Wait. I can't take your money. I still owe the lovely lady…" He stops mid-sentence to calculate. "Seven or eight more churros after today. And by the way, John here has it real bad for you, Miss."

Heat creeps up my neck as I adjust my collar and file the bills back into my jeans pocket.

"Thanks," Summer says, pulling off her sweater and tying it around her hips, revealing a pink tank top that matches her painted toes.

"I know." She catches me staring at her feet. "You expected purple right? But a girl's gotta change things up. You know, to keep a guy guessing." A giggle escapes as she retrieves the paper bag from my hands.

If you could only guess what I'm about to tell you.

"So… what was that about?" Summer asks. "Did you pay him to tell me that you like me every time I buy a churro? That's the third time he's said something."

Looking at Lake Michigan to avoid her eyes and my embarrassment, I ignore her question. Wishing I could stay in this place, I clear my throat and lead Summer to a park bench facing the marina, lots of sailboats out on the water today.

Wanting to change the subject, but not ready to talk about the hard stuff, I think of Talia. "Are you and your sisters close?"

"Close as in nosey, yes. We're in each other's business, and no one goes to bed without telling the rest of us the latest and greatest. All cuz we made a dumb pact when we were tweens."

I made a pact with myself on the way over here: I'm not going to let Dad hurt one more person in my life.

"Want me to tell you?" she asks, pushing her churro back in the bag again.

Shrugging my shoulders, I say, "Sure."

"Okay, but don't say I didn't warn you." Summer looks to the left and right, seeming to make sure we don't have an audience. Then says, "Well, I was ten when I got my period." She pauses to let the word register.

When Talia got hers at age thirteen, Mom was already gone. I just remember her panicking that Dad would kill her for messing up her bed sheets, so together we scrubbed the dark stains out of the cloth before washing them twice, and I thought she had cut her leg or something, but then she threw me a Judy Blume book from her collection and needless to say, we both grew up that week.

"Well, I got my monthly friend, as Mom calls it, and I didn't tell my sibs," Summer says, looking at me without turning her head. "They found out from Mom who made a cake that night and lined the counter with gifts. Get this, the bags were filled with training bras, lip gloss and other make up, and the last one had tampons and pads in it. I didn't want to take the pads out, but

Autumn snagged it from me, saying, 'Show us too! We wanna see what you got!' And the secret was out. The whole family now knew I had come of age or whatever."

I'm looking at the lake, and I don't know how to respond when Summer asks, "Did I say too much?"

"Well, I mean, it's not like you told me what color they were." The bras. I can't say that word.

"Pink. Purple. And Mom even got me a white one with baby blue polka dots!" Summer's laughing. I think she enjoys making me squirm.

Attempting to redirect the conversation away from puberty, I say, "Yeah. So, you and your sisters promised each other something that day?" If I had Summer's porcelain skin, I'd be a nice shade of red right now.

"Winter thought of the idea. Nothing happens with our bodies, boobs, or boys without a sister check-in."

I know she didn't just say the other 'b' word. She did, didn't she? So much for veering away from uncomfortable topics. Looking off to my right, I'm so afraid of where my eyes will land when I turn to face Summer again.

Summer clears her throat. "Mom's a breast cancer survivor. So we had to learn to get checkups pretty early on. Yeah, so you could say, we're all pretty close. And Dad's cool with our girls' nights out. He knows we need each other, and we're all nicer to him when we've vented with each other. They're super over-protective, but they love us. You should come by and meet everyone some time. We could leave out the hitch-hiking thing and just tell them we met at the library. But like I said, don't say I didn't warn you. When you come, be prepared to be on trial. They'll drill you on everything from your kindergarten teacher's name, to what you got on the SATs, to why you want to date me, to how you treat your grandmother."

I decide to ignore the part where Summer said, I want to date her and let her keep talking. And I never took the SATs. And the word trial reminds me why I came. Dad.

"Well, because everyone knows that if a guy treats his grandma nice," Summer says, "He'll treat his girl like a queen."

"I think I've kept you from studying long enough. Shouldn't you get back to your books? I think… I should go."

I look behind us. Somewhere back there lies the library, but Summer stays seated, leaning toward me. "You never told me what happened, really? With your dad, and going down to the police station and everything. Your text was pretty vague."

"How should I say this?" I'm gonna miss watching those cinnamon-coated lips move a mile a minute. "I think we should take a break until I have this all figured out. No point in dragging you into the mess I created." With a napkin from my pocket, I attempt to gently brush the cinnamon from her mouth. It doesn't work.

"So what are you saying?" Summer asks, reminding me I haven't told her much about me.

I need to protect her from Dad. And the only way I can do that is to keep her away from me, so there's no chance Dad will connect us. He'll ruin this, just like he ruined my chances of getting my place and my job back. I don't think telling her more personal things will help us to walk away from each other. Instead I ask her, "Would you still like me if I told you I was in jail last night?"

Before she finishes off her last bite, Summer rubs her hands to brush off powdered sugar. "Come again?"

"I came to say that I might be tied up for a bit and, I guess I didn't want to disappear like last time and not tell you where I went."

I can't tell what boggles my mind more: the fact that Summer shared so many personal stories or the fact that Summer knows I spent the night in jail and still sits here. One thing I do know: walking away is going to be so much harder than I thought.

"It's bad," I say, hoping to encourage Summer to walk away from me.

Summer says, "How bad? Do you need money?"

Even if I don't find a job soon, I would never ask her for money. "You just want me to be indebted in churros to you for life, don't you?"

Summer forces a smile, the cinnamon on her lips sparkling. "Sure. Works for me." But neither of us eats any more now as we rise from the park bench and start back toward the library.

When we arrive at the door, I have the sudden urge to kiss her, but I've never done this before. I wouldn't even know which way to lean. And would she even want to kiss me after everything I just told her? I can't explain it—Summer next to me makes me not so scared of the coming winter. But what I want and what she needs are two different things.

A cinnamon-coated peck makes a surprise landing on my cheek, and Summer's eyes glisten. "Tell me one thing—do you have a roof over your head tonight?"

"I'm working on it..." I say, looking away, dizzy from her kiss.

Worry fills her eyes as Summer asks, "Will you be okay? How will I know if you're okay?" She's forcing a small smile, and if her eyes were seasons, summer turns to fall.

Letting go of her hand to make room for an elderly couple walking in the front door, I decide not to walk her into the library. "I'll call you, okay."

"I'll be right here," she says, spinning on her heels and facing the windows on the second floor. The windows I caught her looking out of. Then she adds, "Wondering. Hoping you're okay. And no matter how bad it gets, no more spontaneous Lake Michigan swims at night. Promise?"

I nod. And this time, I lean forward and plant a kiss on her cheek, bringing summer back to her eyes. And that's how we part. No commitments. Few answers. One promise.

22
~Talia~

The aromas of ginger and cardamom hit me the moment Lagan unlocks his parents' front door and gives my hand a tight squeeze. Then let's go. We're officially in the South Asian, PDA-free zone.

"Hello. Hello. Hello." A silver-haired man wearing a grey sweater vest over his button-down approaches with his arms extended to greet us. He hugs Lagan and brings his hands centimeters from my shoulders and sort of air-pats them, guiding us toward the kitchen. "Come in. Come in. Chai is ready, kids."

Kids? Lagan throws me an eyebrow-raising look, maybe asking me to bear with his parents. Or not to judge him because of his family.

"Oh Beta[1]," the woman wearing a lilac-colored salwar kameez[2] adjusts her chunni[3] when she turns from

---

[1] beta – a term of affection for a child from a parental figure.

[2] salwar kameez – traditional clothes worn by South Asians

[2] salwar kameez – traditional clothes worn by South Asians

91

the stovetop to greet me. "So happy to see and finally meet the lovely Talia. Too bad Lagan's little sister is studying abroad this year. Prima would have loved to meet you too. Do show her in, Lagi-beta."

Lagi-beta? That's cute. "Hi, Mrs. Desai.

"Please. Call me Auntie." Lagan's mom waves me over to her side and gives me a squeeze.

"Okay Mrs., I mean, Auntie."

"Sit down. Sit down," Lagan's dad motions to the dining room table in the adjoining room covered with Indian sweets, tiny triangular samosas, and blue flower-printed Corningware teacups—the same pattern we owned. The same cups that Dad smashed against the counter and then threw at Mom's back. My abs tighten.

"How many sugars do you take in your chai, Beta?" Auntie is asking me, hot tea streaming into the cups.

"No sugar, thanks." I say, folding and unfolding the napkin on the table in front of me.

Lagan's mom looks at me, the spoon of sugar midair and puts it back, a bit of awkward silence filling the air.

"Mom, you made your famous samosas." Lagan puts one on my plate and takes two for himself. "Thanks, Mom. You went all out."

Auntie's smile returns as she sits and stirs her two spoons of sugar in her teacup. I raise the cup to my lips, and when I notice my hand shaking, I return it to the table. Turning the cup till the blue flowers are out of my view, I go back to folding and unfolding my napkin.

"Chutney?" Lagan's dad slides the bowl of minty green sauce toward me.

"Thanks. Uncle." The words sound like a foreign language to me as I break off a little piece of samosa and

---

[3] chunni – long scarf

dab it into the green sauce on my plate. I wait for Lagan to take the first bite and then place a small piece past my lips. Spice fills my senses and without thinking I take a swig of the tea and burn my tongue, dropping the cup to the table with a splash.

Lagan gets up from the table and returns with two cups of ice water, placing one by my plate. My stomach jumps when I feel his hand pat my leg under the table, making me choke on my water. His hand comes up to pat my back as I cough it out, and his mom says, "More chai, anyone? Help me with the chicken, Rajiv. Lagan told me you eat meat, right?"

I manage a nod, unable to make eye contact. Lagan's dad follows his mom to the kitchen, and Lagan covers his mouth like he's holding back a laugh. I step on Lagan's foot under the table.

"Well that went well," I say, taking a bite from a gulab jamun[4] to cool my now spice-inflamed, burnt tongue.

"They love you," Lagan says, placing a whole gulab jamun into his mouth.

"Mom only makes chicken for the special days. For. Special people."

"Sure. I believe you. And the good half-Indian girl isn't even in the kitchen helping."

"Well, you can certainly go and join my mother. I'm sure my dad would love to escape right about now," Lagan says. "But first," And he glances at the doorway to make sure no one's there and plants a kiss on my lips.

As I rise to make my way to the kitchen, a tad giddy, I hear Lagan from behind say, "Just helping you with the living on the edge thing you do."

---

[4] gulab juman – Indian dessert of syrupy-like donuts

Before entering the kitchen, I turn to face Lagan, and that ear to ear smile makes my insides leap. Duty calls.

"Uncle." The word sounds a little less funny with each time I say it. "I can help Auntie if you want?"

"Why thank you, Beta." Uncle doesn't wait for Auntie to protest and passes me, carrying a pot of rice. "The kitchen is all yours."

Alone with Lagan's mom whose back to me makes me feel about as invited as a snowstorm in summertime, I inch my way to the counter. A plaque on the wall reads, "Family First." Another, bordered with a white flower garden, says, "Grace Grows Here." And that's the one that gives me the courage to speak.

"Auntie," I say, still standing a couple feet away, "Who taught you how to cook?"

Stirring meticulously, Lagan's mom says, "Oh, that would be my grandmother. She was the one who told me the secrets of each spice."

Secrets of spice? I like the sound of that. "Your mom didn't cook much?" I ask, making conversation.

"My mother," Lagan's mom pauses, then turns to face me, putting her ladle down on a saucer. "She didn't, how shall I put it, stick around."

My heart sinks. Did Lagan's mom lose her mother like I lost mine? Lagan never said anything of the sort.

"What's your favorite dish to make?" I ask, hoping she won't notice my changing the subject.

"My mother's favorite was ras malai,[5]" Lagan's mom says, stress lines appearing across her forehead. "And that's why I hate it."

I swallow. "I'm sorry to bring her up."

"Don't be," Lagan's mom resumes stirring the curry

---

[5] ras malai – Indian dessert made of ricotta cheese patties in sweet milky sauce.

chicken. "She left my father for another man when I was seven. At the time, I thought I pushed her away for not eating her cooking. I blamed myself for years and even tried to force myself to eat ras malai when it made me gag. But then one day, the year Lagan's father started courting me, he said, 'Why do you torture your tongue with the past? Taste something new. The future needs room.'" She smiles my way and then looks back to her pot.

"He courted you?" I'm curious about this.

"We didn't call it dating, because my grandmother would have put a restraining order on him." She laughs as I turn so she can't see me biting my lip. "He was quite the gentleman. Flowers. Chocolates. And he even made me cassette tapes with love songs on them. Told me to fall asleep to the music so I would dream of dancing with him. First time I ever danced with Uncle was on our wedding day. After the ceremony. After everyone went home. We danced under the New Delhi stars, and I'm sure one or two fell in our honor that night."

I see where Lagan gets his romantic side. Not sure if I should ask, I take a deep breath and say, just above a whisper, "Do you think you could teach me to dance? And a recipe or two? Maybe Lagan's favorite dish?" After Mom died, Dad discarded all the Indian spices and we never ate Indian food at home from that day on.

"Of course." Lagan's mom pulls me over to the counter and opens up her spice tin, just like the one Mom used. "Let me tell you one secret while the boys are in the other room." She takes a pinch of red powder and places it on my palm. "Taste it."

Obeying, I'm careful not to let it linger on my taste buds too long for fear of further damage, but it's not hot, just smoky and flavorful.

"Paprika." Lagan's mother points to the other red

powder, a shade lighter in another tin and says, "Chili powder. Don't ever mix them up or chance another kind of fire breaking out at the dinner table," and we're both laughing and I don't even realize until she repeats herself, like the punch line of a joke, that she said the single word that has reigned havoc on my life in the past weeks. And years. *Fire.*

As we return to the dining room, Lagan and his father are standing in front of the TV in the next room, and from the sound of Lagan's cheer, the Bulls must be on.

"Arr-ay!" Auntie calls to them. "Dinner is ready," and they return. Uncle serves chicken and rice, while Auntie scoops an extra helping of plain yogurt on my plate, winking at me.

Lagan's knee bumps mine and this time I let my hand slip under the table and find his. Running my fingertips over his palm, I make his hand my Post-it tonight. I take my index finger and trace a heart over his and he traces one on mine. Watching Lagan's parents exchange jokes about a grain of rice on his chin or the measure of pickle on her plate fills me somewhere inside. And I haven't even taken my first bite.

23
~Jesse~

Watching the sun dip behind Chicago high-rises outside the window, I ride the train back and forth, the billboards providing no clarity. Posters everywhere display fathers holding hands with, hugging their kids, or tossing them in the air. Frickin' lies.

A plane sails across the sky, scaling toward earth, taunting me at first. Rising to scan the transit map, I exit downtown and transfer to the Blue Line. With each passing stop, more and more passengers enter, rolling luggage in tow.

When the voice overhead announces, "Last stop. O'Hare Airport is the final stop," I let people in a rush to catch flights exit first. Walking up escalators, down corridors and past signs directing travelers to different airlines, I finally spot one that reads Information.

The woman in front of me repeats her question loudly to the guy at the counter. "I said, my luggage never arrived, and I'm late for a meeting. Who takes care of that?"

"I'm sorry, Miss." The guy writes something on the paper in front of him, then slides it over to the woman.

"This is a layout of the airport and you need to take your complaint to the claims department, which is," tapping on a circled area on the page, "right here. That's a couple of terminals over, and I'm sure someone will gladly help you."

Swiping the map off the counter, she storms off, and I can hear her yelling into her phone when the gentleman says, "Next. How can I help you?"

Stepping forward, I clear my throat and say, "Who should I speak with if I'm looking for a job?"

The guy gives me a once-over and pulls out a fresh map of the airport. Before he writes on it, he asks, "What kind of job were you thinking?"

I don't know. I just want to be close to airplanes, pilots, and the sound of take-offs. Thinking of the woman who just left, I say, "Ummm… do you think they need someone to help out on the runway? Maybe load the luggage onto the planes."

"You realize that you'll need security clearance just to apply? And references. And then you'll have to go through security every day you come into work. And it's no walk in the park. Those guys out there have to work through the rain, snow, sleet and storms." He cocks his head to the side. "Sure you can handle it?"

Reference letters? Who's going to refer a guy who got arrested? Even with the charges dropped, I suddenly doubt my chances of ever getting hired by anyone. "Thanks," I say, leaving the map on the counter.

Instead of boarding the train, I follow the cars headed toward the Airport Exit on foot and spot a clearing off the highway ramp, lay on my back, and watch planes fly overhead. The sun's setting now, and I'm guessing the pilots are wearing shades if they're headed west. Hands behind my head, I make up destinations for each flight I spot. Jamaica. California.

Texas. I'm sure one of them is headed to Texas.

Feeling the phone buzz in my pocket, I ignore it, still unsure how I'll break the news to Talia. A second buzz in combination with the chill of the ground causes me to sit up and read the text messages.

Talia's reads, "Lagan told me. You rock!"

I don't have the heart to give her the update.

The second text is from a number I don't recognize: I'm sorry to introduce myself like this, but I know your father. And I want to meet you and your sister.

I stare at the phone, and then quickly rise to my feet and glance around. No one seems to be near enough to me that they're paying any attention to me. As I walk back toward the airport, I type: Who are you? And why should my sister and I meet with a total stranger?

Immediately, a reply comes: I really want to tell you in person. Would you please consider meeting me just one time, so I can properly introduce myself? We can meet in a public place, somewhere you feel comfortable. A restaurant. A park. Navy Pier. You can choose.

No thanks. I hit reply and then send one more text: And leave us alone.

What an idiot.

As I board the train to head back to Lagan's place, those stupid daddy-kid posters seem to be following me, no matter where I sit. Re-reading the mystery texts, I'm glad my last message shut the person up.

One thing I can't shake is the fact that if the person knew anything about me, he'd know better than to mention Dad when he asked me to meet him. *He.* I guess I'm assuming. Come to think of it, if Dad's up to something, he has the brains to warn the person never to mention any connection to himself. So that leaves two possibilities: either the person is stupid or really doesn't know. I'm betting on the latter, but there's only one way to find out for sure.

Typing. Backspace. Typing again. Erasing some more. I stare at the phone and almost reverse my decision.

Then I type: Okay. If you can't tell me who you are, tell me why you have to meet me? A hint. Something?

I wait, and then two words appear.

To apologize.

For what? I message.

Can I share the reason face to face? It won't take much of your time. You tell me when and where to meet you.

Not wanting to get cornered into a lengthy situation, I respond, Ok. Monday morning. 8 AM. By Buckingham Fountain.

Lekker. I'll ride a bike over. I know that spot.

Dismissing the first word as an auto-correct fail, and wanting to remind this stranger that this is not an invitation to hang out, I text: One time. Five minutes.

24
~Jesse~

The wind in Windy City ain't playing around tonight as I make my way back to the college dorms. The streetlights brighten and students lugging backpacks pass me, talking tests and labs and group projects. Spotting blinking lights moving across the black sky above, the airplane heading east is out of my reach, just like my dreams. When this is all over, I wonder if I'll learn how to fly one of those babies. And someday find those purple roses Summer asked for. I want her to know I didn't forget.

On the stairwell up to Lagan and Reggie's room, I stop before exiting on to the sixth floor. I'm not looking forward to telling my sister that we don't have a place. The lounge buzzes with voices and laughter.

"Hey. Jesse's back. Let's see how he weighs in on this debate." Lagan motions for me to join them.

"What?" I see Talia sitting next to Lagan on one couch, Reggie and Rani on another.

"Reg here thinks the next time I get arrested, I should stay long enough to check out the prison gym. Shoot some hoops. School some guys. But that's never gonna happen. I'm just not the criminal type, hello?"

"You did manage to steal my sister's heart," I say, and while everyone laughs, Lagan's eyes lock with Talia's.

"Hey, did you eat?" Reggie directs my attention to the pizza box on the center table.

"I'm okay."

While the others fill plates with pizza slices, Talia comes over and pulls me toward the hallway. "So how'd it go with Summer?"

Avoiding Talia's eyes, I say, "Fine."

"You coulda brought her over to hang out?"

"Not that fine." I look at Talia this time. "We're taking a break. Until the whole trial thing blows over. I think she understands."

"Okay. I guess. What about the place you mentioned? When do we move in?"

"About that..." I hate disappointing her. "It didn't work out, but I promise I'll keep looking. And I'll find something else for us, okay?"

"I know." Talia glances over her shoulder. "You know I meant to tell you, but I saw him. I saw Dad at the precinct, the night you got arrested."

"Why didn't you tell me?"

"I meant to. It's just you were out, and everyone was happy. I didn't want to talk about one more hard thing." Talia leans in and pulls my forehead to hers. "I don't know what I'd do without you. I'm grabbing a slice for you to eat so we can walk and catch up. Cool?"

"Yeah. That's cool," I say, and I can hear Talia telling Lagan that we'll be right back.

Lagan moves past me into his room and comes out, tosses both Talia and me Bulls sweatshirts, and says, "The just-in-case factor."

Reggie's up getting more pizza. "In which case, you

need to hand her an umbrella and give the dude your Bulls Poncho. Just in case."

Rani's stares at her phone before refuting Reggie. "Zero percent chance of precipitation, all. I think you can skip the rain gear."

Just the mention of a poncho makes me think of Summer. When this is all over, I'll hunt around for a poncho with purple flowers.

25
~Talia~

It's not cool enough for a sweatshirt, but I pull Lagan's over my head and inhale deeply. As we walk, I tell Jesse about my brief talk with Dad, and how our grandparents are probably dead.

"Figures."

"Maybe," I say, "But it hasn't all been bad." I'm thinking Lagan and now the friendships with Reggie and Rani, and I hope he's able to think of at least Summer.

"Before I forget, Luke called." Jesse turns to face me as I explain. "He said they're hashing out a plea bargain so we won't have to go to trial. It would end the whole thing once and for all. Luke says they're trying to work out reasonable terms. So this is a pretrial hearing we have to attend. No jury. Just our lawyers and the judge."

"What terms? Doesn't that mean he gets off easy?"

"Luke assured me that even with a reduced sentence, Dad would spend plenty of years behind bars. But we wouldn't have to testify in front of a courtroom of strangers." That's the part that appeals to me.

"What time?" Jesse asks.

"It starts at nine on Wednesday, but Luke said to

arrive at the courthouse at 8:30AM so he can prep us on what to expect, etc."

"So no need to practice talking on the witness stand?" Jesse asks.

"Well, that's still on." I'm remembering Luke's exact words. "He said, we prepare like we're going to trial until the judge says we're not going to trial. My appointment with Luke is on Monday. You need to call and schedule yours. So don't forget."

We continue to walk alongside each other across the Lakeshore underpass over to Lake Michigan. When my brother stops, I stand next to him, and we stare out at the dark waters. Minutes pass and a question that has burned in me for the last day returns to me.

"So what was that night like in prison, Jess?" I never wanted to ask him for details in front of everyone.

Jess shrugs his shoulders. "I fell asleep so the bed couldn't have been that bad."

"Okay, I'll drop it."

More time passes, and we remain quiet, avoiding eye contact.

"Well, there was this one thing." Jesse looks over his shoulder, turns and continues. "Do you ever have dreams that stop in the middle? Like a solid wall drops out of the sky and keeps you from moving to whatever happens next?"

Only one. I'm guessing it's the same dream. "The one where you fall. I always wake up right before you fall off the roof."

Jesse looks off to the lake again. Shaking his head, he says, "That sucks." He pauses then says, "That's not the one I'm talking about."

Twirling my hair with my fingers, I wait for him to say more.

"There's this one when Mom took us to the beach."

"The time we tried to run away?"

"No," Jess says. "It's weird, in this dream, I was really small and you were like five or something. It was your birthday."

My gut contracts. I know what day he's referring to.

"I get to this part of the dream when Mom pushes us in a stroller up the edge of the water and then the dream ends. Every time."

How do I say it? Looking at my brother's hands at the back of his neck, I picture them flailing in the water. "You can't remember because you blacked out."

Jesse turns to me, confusion in his eyes.

Swallowing, I look away and tell him the truth. "Mom pushed the stroller into the water."

"Why? She knew I didn't know how to swim...unless... I don't believe it." Jesse throws a punch at an invisible enemy, turns and walks away from me.

I race up behind him. "Wait. You have to hear the rest."

"I've heard enough," Jesse says, quickening his pace. "Forget I asked."

Pulling at his shirt, I force Jesse to slow down, but he turns abruptly, forcing me to let go of his back. "What? Now you want to defend her. I'm tired of making excuses for her. I just want to forget her, okay."

"Fine. Let me tell you the rest of the story. Then you can forget her. Forget everything." We both know we'll never forget, but I need Jesse to hear me out.

Jesse kicks the grass, but he stays.

"I've thought about that day so many times, trying to make sense of what Mom was thinking. All I remember is screaming as I clawed my way out of the stroller in the water before it went completely under and grabbing Mom's hair to keep my head above water. Someone off shore must have heard the commotion, because a stranger pulled me out and plopped me next to you lying on the sand. And all I had left in my hands was a strand of Mom's hair. The stranger left us on the beach and returned after pulling the stroller and then Mom out too, and then he did CPR on you, Jess. He saved your life, and I didn't even know his name."

"Mom shoulda gone to jail," Jesse says, walking away again.

"Mom already lived in prison," I say to his back.

Jess stops in his tracks, and his shoulders start to tremble.

"She was stuck, Jess." Closing the gap, I wrap my arms around my brother's back. "She thought she was saving us." Jess's chest heaves in my arms, and I weep silently onto his back.

Clearing my throat, I close the chapter of this story with one last thing. Something I need to hear too. "I don't know much, but I'm sure of one thing, Jess. And even if you don't believe it, I do. Mom loved us."

26
~Talia~

When we return to the dorms, I ask Lagan, "About tonight?"

"Take my bed again," he says, no hesitation. "The suite has a few couches. Jesse can crash there too. Or take Reg's bed." Cupping my face in his chocolate brown hands right before we get to the door, he says, "We'll work it out, okay."

I thank him and climb up into bed. Exhausted from the last couple of days, my eyes shut, and I fall asleep with ease. In my dreams, I expect to visit the beach. Mom. The world Jesse and I just revisited.

Instead, I'm back in the garden where the gardener speaks with the woman whose bleeding stopped. He's still scattering the shiny seeds everywhere. I'm close enough to hear them talk, but it's like they don't see me.

"What kind of seeds are they?" the woman asks.

"Think of all those who brighten your days."

The woman shakes her head. "If the sky is my life, there should only be a few stars... at times, only one. You."

The gardener runs his hand over the sky and several

stars stream across, blazing out of sight. "I'm not a star, my dear. But I'll always be with you."

"How will I find you?" the woman asks, sounding frantic as the gardener walks away.

"Follow the stars."

"But what about nights when the clouds blot out the stars?" She's searching the sky now, but he's gone. No more questions. And no more answers.

27
~Talia~

The weekend passes by and I see little of Jess. But each night he comes home, a little more mopey than the last. Still no job. And no place for us to stay. I remind him, no one's around on the weekend. We can both try when Monday arrives. And for now, Lagan's not in any rush for us to leave.

While Lagan spends time reading for his upcoming semester, I journal the story of my life. What I can remember of it. Luke told me writing it down will help to formulate my thoughts when I'm on the witness stand, in case the plea bargain, pre-hearing, doesn't go as hoped. Like the Great Wall of China, Mom's death divides my memories. After Friday night's walk with Jesse, I just hope my brother can move past the things he can't change so he can begin pursuing his future.

And at least once a day, Reggie tries to make us play Orgo-formula Pictionary, but only Rani takes the bait. No one has to spell it out. Seems pretty clear that these two enjoy spending time together.

Waking up Monday morning, Lagan waits by the dorm stairs with his backpack and Bulls cap on.

Jesse left before I woke up, and Reggie took off to study. "Where you headed?" I ask Lagan.

"Wherever you're going. After you." Lagan holds the door open.

As I pass him, I'm tickled he wants to be my bodyguard. "You know you don't have to go everywhere I go. I'll be fine."

"Well, where's the lawyer's office?" Lagan pulls out his phone to map it as I read him the address off Luke's business card. "That's right next to a Rite Aid, and I need to restock on toothpaste and razor blades." He rubs the stubble on his jawline.

"And Post-its?" I bump him playfully on the stairs, knowing full well that there's a Rite Aid down the street.

Lagan pats the side of his backpack. "Nope. Still good."

When we arrive at the building, I turn to hug Lagan goodbye. He circles me around while still holding me in his arms and points inside a window to the couch across from the elevator. "Let's meet up there when you're done." A nod. A peck on the lips. And I walk through the door in search of Suite 468.

Luke's waiting for me. "Let's get right down to business. At the pre-hearing, chances are you won't have to say a word. But the judge might ask you a few questions. And if this goes to trial, you'll have no choice but to take the witness stand. So we'll do a practice run of what the defense might ask you."

Luke pauses and I force a small smile, but my insides cramp. "Talia, I've worked with many survivors. Trust me when I say this won't be easy. Think before you answer. Keep your answers short. And anytime you don't know the answer, you have the right to refrain. Your goal is to tell the truth, not predicting what might have happened or could happen in the future. Ready?"

RAJDEEP PAULUS

I nod. And the first several questions are easy. Name, age, relationship to the defendant.

Then Luke asks, "When you think back to your chores growing up, did you ever iron your father's shirts?"

I nod, but Luke tells me, "Say the word, 'Yes,'" so I do.

"Would you consider yourself clumsy?"

I shake my head and say, "No. Well, sometimes."

"Did your father ever beat you? Did he ever use violent force against you?"

"Beat, no. Well, I mean, force? I don't know? Is burning considered force?"

Luke's questions keep coming. "Did you ever do the dishes?"

"Yes."

"Who managed the cooking once your mother was out of the picture?"

"Me."

"Did you make your dad tea daily?"

"Yes. I mean, usually. Sometimes, once in a while, he came home late."

"Yes is sufficient. Did your mother love your father? Did you ever see them share a moment? Did he ever hurt you before your mother died? Did he ever say things to hurt you? Verbally abuse you? Threaten you? Call you terrible names?"

"I don't know." My heart's racing. "And I don't know why, but he threatened us with the words, 'or else,' and I...I still hate hearing those words."

"Or else what?"

"He never said."

"Then how did you know it would be bad?"

"I just knew."

"Did you ever witness your dad hurt your mother?"

112

"No. I mean yes."

"Yes or no? Be clear. Be precise."

"Yes. Once." My hands feel sweaty.

"Did you ever see him hurt your brother?"

"No."

"So why do you think your brother or your mother were abused."

"I saw her body. And his back." I focus on Luke's voice so I won't picture my mother's broken body.

"Let's try it again." Luke turns over the board that's been lying upside down on the table, exposing a newspaper clipping. His face stares up at me smiling. *Dad.*

"What's he doing here?"

"He'll be there. You have to be able to tell the truth. Not just to me. But to the whole court. In front of him. With the jury all staring at you."

"How do I do it?" If I close my eyes, I see Mom. If I leave them open, Dad's there. I'm screwed.

"Does it help to look just at me? Start by looking at me."

But I can't. Like a magnetic trance, Dad's stare holds me prisoner, and my tongue feels suddenly like it's in the way. And if my words had feet, I'm stumbling all over the room, knocking over every house of cards Luke spent all afternoon building with me.

"It wasn't that bad. I'm...uh...okay. I'll be...fine. It's all a... ummm... mistake. I'm. The. Mistake."

"What are you saying, Talia?" I hear Luke's question, but fear seizes me, and I'm hiding my left arm under my right, but I can't fully hide. And I can't back up any further in my chair. And the paper hasn't moved, but I feel like he's close. And he could hurt me. He would hurt me if I dare tell what really happened. I can't burn again.

"I can't. I don't want to." I cover his face with my hands, but when I move them, he's still there. Smiling. Like he's already won. And then I hear my mother's words from my dream, and as I rise from the table and move toward the door, the words leave my lips as if they're mine. "Why bother?"

"We'll try again next week. Okay?" Luke asks.

"Maybe we won't have to." I'm thinking of the plea bargain. The pre-hearing is scheduled for Wednesday.

"Maybe." Luke pours himself some coffee from the small carafe on his desk. "It's Gerard Vanderbilt we're dealing with. And his lawyer knows how to play hardball. If they agree to everything we put on the table, Wednesday will go smoothly. We need to be ready for anything."

I'm the last person he needs to remind. I just can't see how it will be any easier next week.

"And Talia," Luke says, his voice gentle. "With some practice, you'll find something to focus on—something that will give you the courage to speak up. I'm sure of it."

Courage is what I asked for.

"And one last thing," Luke says, and I look up, eye to eye with the man who wants me to try again. "Mark Twain once said, 'Courage is not the absence of fear. It is acting in spite of it.'"

"What if, on that day, what if I can't find my brave?"

"I think you should consider a different question. And you might find the answer to that question." Luke says.

"What's that?"

"How different will your life be when this case is over? This is just a bridge. And I'm here to help you get across, okay?"

I nod, leave Luke's office, take the elevator to the

first floor, and meet Lagan in the lobby.

"How'd it go?"

"How'd it go?" I repeat Lagan's question, picturing the words Luke left me with. I'm standing on one side. A bridge. But Dad stands a few feet from me, shaking his head, matches in his hands.

28
~Jesse~

The phone buzzes under my pillow. Not recognizing the number, I ignore the call. A text follows shortly after from the same number:

Everything still good for meeting this morning?

Noting that it's a little before seven, I message, I'll be there, and quietly climb down from Reggie's loft to keep from waking up my sister.

Taking a Post-it from Lagan's desk, I write: T. Hope it goes well with Luke today. I'll set mine up soon. J

With no place to stay and no job right now, I feel stupid for blowing twelve bucks on a cab, but I can't be late and miss meeting this stranger. Handing the bills to the driver, I exit and walk east toward Lake Michigan, over the bridge and pause at the train tracks but the stranger doesn't seem within my view, so I march on.

The first time I see him, my head does a double take. He looks a tad out of place, wearing a scarf around his neck, a grey Roots sweatshirt over his shorts. He has on a black bike helmet and dark shades, and he's sitting next to the fountain cross-legged, fiddling with a pen in his hand as he reads the paper, maybe doing a crossword puzzle. I guess I thought I'd beat him here.

Another biker passes from behind me and never stops, making me question if I have the right person, even though I'm a good twenty feet from facing the man on the bench. The female cyclist sails off down Lakeshore Drive, not even looking back, but I watch her until she's past a bend in the road and completely out of sight. Turning back to the man on the bench, he's gone! What?

Spinning around, I spot him by the bike racks, drinking from his water bottle and dislodging a bike away from the other blue bikes. But instead of riding off, he walks the bike toward me. "Justice?" He asks, pulling off his shades and helmet to shake my hand.

I'm frozen and speechless. I know right away it's no coincidence that he's tall, sports a neat buzz cut and has hazel green eyes. And that jawline—it totally mirrors mine. Like I'm looking at a picture of a younger, stronger, version of Dad, I can't stop staring, and I don't know whether to throw a punch or run away.

"I'm your dad's—"

"I know who you are." I don't but I can guess. "You're related to Dad, aren't you? And you're here to apologize for showing up. Late."

"I'm your Uncle, and I am here to apologize. That part is true." His South African accent confirms my suspicions. And his mouth even looks just like Dad's, but I don't know that I've ever seen Dad wearing a getup like this guy.

"Forget it," I say, walking away. "We never needed you then. We certainly don't need you now." Besides, why would anyone related to Dad want anything to do with the kids Dad hates?

"Your dad's my older brother…" I can hear his voice rising as I walk further away. "He never told me.

117

He never told any of us that he had kids."

I stop in my tracks. Of course he didn't. But why? Why hide us from his family? Then it occurs to me: he wasn't just hiding us. I turn to face this stranger. "When's the last time you saw him or spoke to him?"

"A few days ago. When I paid his bail," he says, and that's all I need to hear. It's obvious whose side he's on. I turn back around and take off running, and just as luck would have it, he catches up. On his bike, pedaling to the pace of my run and talking at the same time.

"Look, I don't expect anything from you. I just wanted to meet my nephew and niece. Geri left us over twenty-five years ago. He cut us off. Before last week, my big brother was dead for all I knew. But he contacted me, and I came. I just couldn't believe it was him. And when I went to pay his bail—"

I stop running, panting as I push his bike away from me. Dad's brother's bike crashes to the concrete ground, and he's pulling himself out from under the wheel, brushing dirt off his clothes, but stays seated on the sidewalk.

"Why would you give a penny to him? Do you have any idea what kind of monster he is?" I want to spit in the face that resembles my father, and I turn once again to leave the jerk on the floor.

But he catches up to me, this time pulling his bike alongside him. "Wait. Just give me two minutes to explain. I just need to tell you one more thing."

I've heard enough. He obviously has no common sense. To just show up after all this time and think his brother could be trusted? Who does that? "Save it," I say. "I have to get somewhere." Forget calling Luke. I just want to get away from this creep. Get away from everybody.

"Geri wants me to talk to you. To tell you we can all

sit down and sort this thing out. He's your father. Give him a chance is all I'm asking."

Really? I stop one last time. "If he sent you here to convince me to stay silent in court, tell my father I'd rather, frickin' chew on rusted nails than let him get away with one more thing."

"That's what I'm trying to tell you." He moves fast and blocks my way with his bike. "I went to pay the bail for my brother and when the clerk asked for the last name, I said 'Vanderbilt,' and he said, 'Which one?' I assumed you were some random person, coincidentally bearing the same surname. But then the clerk slipped and said, 'I've only seen this twice since I started working here.' I asked, 'What?' And he said, 'A father-son duo in jail within days of each other.' Then he quickly apologized for letting his mouth 'run off,' as he phrased it. That's when I knew. I had no idea you were in jail. Nor that you were my nephew. That I have a niece. We've got to sort this out. It's too late for Geri and our father, but it isn't too late for you and your dad."

"You have no idea who he is or what he's capable of," I say, looking down at my phone. I need to go.

"I just want answers," he says. "I think I deserve to hear both sides of the story."

"Seriously?" I shake my head at this man's ignorance. "And what? You expect everyone to just drop everything and fill you in on what's been happening for the last couple of decades. No thanks." I walk around the bike and throw up my hand in the air, lifting a choice middle finger to say goodbye. He doesn't follow.

Back to same old same old. Or as Talia says: Same old. Same cold.

29
~Talia~

Tuesday comes and goes and Jesse is nowhere to be seen, busy job hunting and searching for a place. I spend most of the day journaling more, reminding myself I probably won't have to say a word at the plea bargain hearing. That's the only thing fueling my brave.

Rani knocks on Lagan's door bright and early Wednesday morning. "Talia? I brought you a few things. Just in case."

"Coming," I say, climbing down the loft steps to unlock the door.

Rani's wearing a dark purple business suit, similar to the one she wore the day I first met her, her eyes outlined with a matching purple. "Here," she says, shoving some clothes on hangers toward me. "You have to look the part. And I plugged in my curling iron in the girls' bathroom, so let's get to it."

Draping the clothes over Lagan's chair, the outfits are jacket-skirt combos in rusty orange, dark grey, and poppy red. Setting the red one aside, Lagan obviously didn't get to fill Rani in on my favorite colors. Nothing in the pile is green or blue. Cradling my toiletries and the towel Reggie lent me, I decide a shower will give me time to work through my anxiety over a new wardrobe.

As Rani blow-dries my hair, she hums to herself. Before she starts throwing in curls, Rani pins up half my hair with a sparkly silver hair clip, reminding me of a day so long ago. Mom, Jesse and I shared wishes with each other once, knowing they would never come true. Jesse wished for video games, the ones kids at school raved about. Mom wished for pretty things for her hair. Smoothing out the red skirt over the tan colored stockings Rani brought me, I'm smiling at this temporary wish come true. My wish was for pretty clothes, and when I stand to examine myself in the bathroom mirror, I look like I'm ready to run for President. Running over Dad will do.

Stepping into the black heels, also Rani's, they're a bit big, and I steady myself against the door before exiting the girls' room, deciding to practice in the hallway so I don't trip and ruin the perfectly confident entrance into the courtroom I'm planning. So absorbed in placing one foot in front of the other, I hear Lagan's whistle before I notice him watching me, and heat flushes my cheeks.

"I suppose my face matches this outfit now," I say, tucking my bottom lip under the top one.

"Red is…" Lagan pauses. "My new favorite color."

"You're such a goofball." I walk past Lagan to keep practicing, but he catches my arm and gently turns me to face him. "What if I were wearing orange?"

"I like orange," Lagan says, pulling on a curled lock of my hair and releasing it to bounce back in place. "Pretty."

"What if this shirt were green with purple polka dots?"

Lagan closes the gap between us and says, "I'm sure

I could come up with a plan to hide you."

Pushing him back, I tug on his blue striped tie. "Now if you had a green and purple polka dot tie on, I'd just wrap it around your neck and put you under a tree."

"So you're asking Santa for me. For Christmas?" Lagan's grin has that dimple in full effect.

"Umm, more like, hiding you under a willow tree, you know where moss and fungus grow." Straightening his tie, I pat Lagan's shoulders. "Sorry. Just practicing being courageous. How am I doing so far?"

"Not bad. Rani!" Lagan calls down the hallway. "Did you bring red lip stuff?"

"Red!" The red clothes are enough. I shake my head, but Rani walks toward us, fishing in her purse, and hands me two different tubes.

"Just try it. I think it could be the punch in your one-two smashing outfit."

"Or I could look like a clown, just a little better dressed."

Jesse comes out of the guys' bathroom, dressed like he's going to a wedding, wearing a red tie that matches my clothes.

"Wow," I say, thrilled to see my brother all spiffed up, although the suit is a tad large on him. Lagan is clearly taller, but standing next to each other, they look like a couple of guys ready to light up the night. Except that it's not even eight in the morning.

"Ready?" Reggie folds his own jacket collar back, and smiles at Rani, and I'm still staring at my brother.

"I'll meet you guys there." Jesse leaves without warning.

Not fazed by my brother's quick exit, Rani ushers us toward the stairs. "Let's grab a quick bite, and get moving."

Lagan folds my hand over the lipstick, and leans in

so no one else can hear, "About the lip stuff, whatever you decide is fine. You know I love your lips just the way they are."

Blushing for the second time this morning, I leave him to grab my bag from his room. Rani finds me and hands me a small red hand purse. "Just put your I.D. in there with the lipstick. And you'll be fine."

The only card I have with my photo is my college I.D. I think Dad kept our legal docs in a bank safe. Fishing my I.D. out of my satchel, some Post-its and a pen, I also retrieve the book I taped back together. The book Lagan gave me back in high school. I tore out nearly every page one day at the shelter. I needed to find Mom's strand of hair. It's gone. Forever. Now the book, *A Beautiful Fight*, looks like the willow tree, barely holding itself together. And it doesn't fit either, too wide for the small red pocketbook.

Rani sees me holding the book in one hand and the purse in the other. "Is it like a good luck charm?" she asks, and then I remember the necklace.

"No," I say, finding the blue heart glass pendant Jesse gave me. "But this is," I say, and Rani helps me to clasp the chain behind my neck. Putting the book back, and tucking the heart under my blouse, I attempt a confident smile. "Ready."

30
~ Talia ~

Lagan watches me pace back and forth in front of the courthouse as I nearly trip several times in the heels Rani lent me. She and Reggie went inside to find the waiting room. Jesse has two minutes to get here. One now. We can't be late to the pre-trial hearing. Knowing Dad, he'd find a way to use this to get his case thrown out if he could.

"Let's go!" Jesse says, racing past me through the revolving door before I can chew him out.

Catching up to my brother, I slow him down to a walking pace with a firm grip on his bicep. "Where were you?"

"Later," he says, and Luke meets us head on, directing our steps to the courtroom, his tightened jaw suggesting he is not happy.

"Luke was supposed to brief you." I say right before the officer in uniform opens the doors to the courtroom.

Jesse looks me square in the eyes and says, "It's fine. Let's go."

Lagan grazes a kiss on my forehead. He'll wait out in

the hallway. I follow my brother and Luke, the court buzzing with the previous trial just wrapping up, and we take our seats in an empty row a few rows from the back. Luke drums quietly on his laptop case. Jesse fiddles with his tie. I doodle on Post-its, drawing a tree. Branches. Then two leaves, hanging on at the end of winter. Just as I outline a dewdrop on the tip of one of the leaves, Jesse nudges me, making my pen slip off the Sticky Note, just missing my skirt. Our turn is up.

"All rise. The honorable Judge Nadine Waters presiding." Everyone stands and then when the judge takes her seat, the clerk directs us to take our seats.

Before I can cross my legs, the judge says, "Will the parties of State vs. Vanderbilt approach the bench?" the judge says, from the raised platform, her fiery orange hair falling on her black robed shoulders.

The State Prosecutor's scuffed, black dress shoes make a squeaking sound when he rises next to us to approach the bench. The red of his tie matches my outfit. His subtle nod as he passes by seals the deal. He's fighting for us.

Jesse and I follow a half step behind Luke as Dad's lawyer walks next to Dad down the opposite aisle. When Dad turns to make eye contact, I shift too quickly and bang my knee against the wooden rows. Ouch.

We take our seats in the first row and the judge starts the hearing. "In the case of State vs. Vanderbilt, the documents before me state that the prosecution has proposed a plea bargain? Counsel, would you please read the terms aloud?" She's looking right at the State Attorney.

"Of course, your honor." Prosecutor Tim Driscoll, Luke assures us, is the best of the best. "Yes, the defendant has agreed to a guilty plea accompanied with a reduced sentence. In addition, restitution monies will be paid for the next ten years in conjunction with college tuition, costs for housing apart from the defendant, and all attorney and courtroom fees."

While I mentally assess all Dad promises today to stop this case from going to trial, Judge Waters says, "Defense. Please state your consent."

"Thank you, your honor." Dad's lawyer pushes the spectacles up on his face, his brown goatee a lot bushier than Lagan's closely shaved one. "Yes, but we'd like to alter some details and add one more thing, your honor."

Of course, there's always one more thing with Dad. I steal a glance at Dad, and he's got an ever so subtle smirk on his face, making me all the more nervous.

"Go on. State your proposal, Counsel." Judge Waters leans back, her arms resting on the open folder of papers. Attorney Driscoll straightens his tie, and I'm wondering if he wants to take it off. Perhaps to strangle Dad's team for changing what was already agreed upon.

Dad's lawyer opens up his folder, walks over and hands a paper to the Prosecution, and then the judge. Standing next to Dad again, he clears his throat. "My client will also pay for any medical costs involved in restoring the health of his children, including any plastic surgery fees, medical follow up, prescriptions, and counseling sessions. He wants to assure his children that he is truly remorseful and wishes only for their best future from this day forward. There is no limit on the amount he will pay to see this happen. He also agrees to go to anger management classes and see a psychiatrist for a minimum of a year in replacement of the reduced sentence, based on studies of success rates that far outweigh those of incarcerated individuals."

"Excuse me your honor," Luke speaks up. "The defendant agreed to the reduced sentence, not the elimination of jail time altogether." Luke voices what

I'm thinking.

Before the judge can respond, Jesse's voice rises above the commotion. "You think a little plastic surgery can just erase the past and make it all better?" I grab hold of my brother's arm, but he's too busy glaring at Dad to look at me.

"Absolutely not." Attorney Driscoll says and rips the agreement in half. "No deal."

Luke motions with his right hand for Jesse to stop talking as the judge hits the gavel on her desk. "Order in the court."

"I want to apologize for having you arrested, Justice," Dad says, dismissive of the judge's instructions but speaking tenderly like he means it. "I just wanted to see you. And Talia. I miss—"

"I said, order in the court!" The judge hits her gavel again, and Luke tries to direct Jesse backward to sit down.

Instead, Jesse takes a step toward Dad. "If you think you're not going to jail, you're out of your frickin' mind!" Jesse pushes Luke's hands off and storms out of the courtroom.

All the while, the judge pounds her gavel, screaming, "Order! That's it! The court will go to recess. NOW! Counsel, meet me with your clients in my office in five minutes. Separately. Dismissed."

Avoiding Dad, I run down the aisle after Jesse, out into the corridor past Lagan who catches up with me, followed by Rani and Reggie.

"Over so soon?" Rani asks, slightly out of breath.

"Did you see which way Jesse went?" I ask Lagan.

"How'd it go?" Reg asks, but I look past him down the hallway.

"We have to be in the judge's office in five minutes. I need to find Jesse. Now."

"I'll check the front of the building," Lagan says.

"And I'll check the men's room." Reggie turns the other way and walks quickly back to the waiting area.

"Want to try calling him?" Rani asks, holding out her phone. "Or texting him?"

I'm nodding, but I can't think straight. What's the number? Rani punches a message into her phone, and Luke approaches, case under his arm, wiping his face with his free hand.

"I'm sorry," I say when Luke stops in front of me.

"Would have helped if your brother had showed up to be briefed. At the very least, I could have emphasized the importance of maintaining his composure." Luke's looking over my shoulder. "Where is he?"

Rani's phone buzzes and just as she finishes saying, "They're on their way. He's with Lagan," I spot them coming in, Lagan following Jesse, a scowl plastered on my brother's face.

Luke moves past us to meet Jesse and pulls him off to the side to talk with him alone, then motions for me to join them. As I pass Lagan, his hand brushes mine and his eyes mirror mine. Cloudy with a chance of more storms to come. Sigh.

"Let's get one thing straight." Luke's looking at Jesse, but talking to both of us as we find our way to the judge's office. "I, alone, do the talking."

I nod. Jesse looks away.

"Do I make myself clear?" Luke asks. "Because I know Judge Waters' style. She'll hold you in contempt if you ever do that again and if you get thrown out, the case can get thrown out. So do we have a deal? No more target practice at our own toes?"

We follow Luke to the judge's quarters, and he asks us if we agree to forget the plea bargain and move to trial. We do. The hallways are decorated with portraits of courtroom scenes, famous trials over the years, and some faces show triumph and some disappointment. When we reach Judge Waters' office, Jesse mutters an apology to Luke right before he knocks on the door.

"She'll be with you shortly," the admin on a phone lowers it to say, then resumes her conversation.

After about a minute, the double doors open and Dad and his lawyer exit the judge's office, Dad's head high and a small smile curved on his mouth. Jesse's back stiffens and the two of them make eye contact, neither looking away.

"See you in court," Luke says after they pass us, and we enter the office.

"Sit down, please," Judge Waters says, sporting a soft yellow blouse, her black robe hanging on a coat rack next to her wide oak desk.

As each of us takes a seat, Luke clears his throat. Maybe a reminder to keep our mouths shut.

"Well," the Judge waits a beat then says, "We'll reschedule the pre-hearing or we'll just move to set a date for trial. What will it be, Counselor?"

"My clients move to go to trial, thank you," Luke says, giving both Jesse and me a quick glance to make sure we're still in agreement. We both nod simultaneously.

"I understand that this case isn't easy for any of the parties involved," Judge Waters says. "But I need your clients to understand that if they continue to talk out of turn in a federal court of law, they will be held in contempt, and no matter how true their stories might be, they will neither count nor be heard. Have I made myself clear?" She's looking right at Jesse.

"Can I say something?" Jesse asks, Luke rising to his feet.

"I'll discuss my client's question with him when we

leave. And we're leaving, now." Luke cocks his head toward the door, but Judge Waters motions with her hands for Luke to sit back down. He does.

Judge Waters folds her hands and waits for Jesse to speak.

"I'm sorry for the outburst earlier."

"Apology accepted." Her smile reveals facial lines on her cheeks and crow's feet by her eyes. What I wouldn't give to have seen my own mother age.

"But," Jesse adds. "There was a time when I stopped talking. I couldn't speak up against my dad even when I wanted to. I can now. And I, just, I don't want him to think I'm afraid of him anymore. I want to make that clear."

"The best way to do that is to tell your story the right way. At the right time." Judge Waters rises from her desk now. "I have to get back into court. But I think you understand. And Counsel Barrons here will walk you through the best way to tell your story in court. Six months from now. I'll see you then." And she puts on her robe and as we walk out the double doors, she heads through a side door, maybe a private passageway to the courtroom.

"We'll meet in a couple of weeks, okay," Luke says to me. Jesse's looking at his phone, earning him a nudge in the back from me. "Keep thinking about what I said, okay. We need character witness statements and today is just a small taste of what kind of surprises your Dad's team will try to pull. Look at me, both of you." Luke waits till Jesse looks up. "Six months will fly by, so you can't lose your resolve to put this man behind bars. He'll pull out all the stops to prove he's a good father. Or he didn't mean to hurt you. Or he's committed to changing his ways. And a whole lot of other excuses he'll come up with to get out of jail time and keep this from tarnishing his record. We have to do our part and be ready for each and every lie he comes up with. Let's schedule a meeting for next week, Friday at 1:00pm. And Jesse, show up on time or don't bother. But just know that when the day of your trial comes, if you decide to be late, you're pretty much asking the judge to set your dad free."

~31~
Talia

We're at the revolving door entrance now. "Take care, you two," Luke says, and I follow my brother outside after texting Lagan that I'll meet him back at his place later.

"Okay, Jesse," I say, trying to keep up with my brother who's marching ahead of me. "Slow down and tell me something."

"I have to get a job." Jesse's looking down at his phone again. "We need money to pay the lawyer. We need money to feed ourselves. And we'll need money to pay the rent once I find a place."

"I get that." I tug at my brother's jacket sleeve. "Just stop for a minute. Let's talk. What happened back there?"

Jesse turns to face me. "What do you mean, what happened? There was no way I was letting Dad get off scot-free. And then he idiotically apologizes for having me arrested. How about saying sorry for the countless times he burned me?"

I inch the sleeve up on my left arm. My scarred and deformed skin looks more ugly to me some days than other days. Today's one of those days.

Reaching to touch the bumpy skin, Jesse pulls my sleeve down instead. "I'll become a pilot. Make a ton of money. And I'll fly you to the best plastic surgeon in the world and I'll...we'll fix this."

"What if I don't want it fixed? What if I need it to remind me to never let my guard down again?"

Jesse stuffs his hands in his dress pants pockets, and I walk on with him, wondering where Dad gets off thinking oodles of cash can make up for the past. Wanting to cheer up my little brother, I say, "You should still learn to fly a plane," happy to talk about something else. "Can I help you with the pilot school application? Maybe there's an essay you have to write to tell them why you wanna learn to fly?"

"If you know how to drive a car," says a stranger from behind us. "It can't be much different from flying a plane. Maybe easier."

The man has a distinct accent, but even before I finish turning to face him, Jesse grabs my arm and says, "Let's go."

"Wait," the man says, "Can I just show you one picture. A photo taken when your dad and I were kids."

I stop. Did he just say—? "Who are you?" I say, eye to eye with the man now, but the answer is written on his face. He looks so much like Dad, just younger.

"I said, 'Let's go.'" Jesse stands between me and the man, once again trying to direct my steps away.

"I won't take much time." The man talks directly to me. "Let me tell you one story. The reason why your father left South Africa. And after that, I won't ever bother you again."

His accent is South African, and his eyes are the same hazel green as Dad's. And mine.

As I reach for the picture he's holding out, Jesse

133

snags it and rips it in half. And then he drops the torn photograph and steps on it. "We don't want your stories. We don't know you and we don't want to know you!" Then Jesse turns to me and says, "I don't trust this guy. He paid Dad's bail. He's not a friend. Are you coming with me or not?"

The man bends down to pick up the ripped picture, and says, "What did Geri do to make you hate him so much? If you don't want to hear my story, will you at least tell me yours?"

Jesse's angry stare magnetically pulls at me, but I hear Dad's brother's words and I can't explain it, but a little part of me wants to give him a chance. Jesse walks away, no interest in story time, and I see this stranger's eyes on me, pleading for something. Anything.

I turn to see how far ahead Jesse is. He's stopped less than twenty feet from me. He's waiting, but I want to know one thing. "What's your name?" I ask, already several steps away from Dad's brother.

"William. But growing up, my friends always called me Billy." He looks in my eyes when he says, "You can call me, Uncle Billy, if you like?"

Slipping off Rani's heels and stringing the back straps between my thumb and pointer finger, I walk backwards away, barefoot. "When you see Dad, why don't you ask him to tell you a story or two? Then we'll talk."

32
~Talia~

When I catch up with Jesse, it hits me that "Uncle" Billy met my brother already.

"Hey!" I say and Jesse sees my bare feet and stops to wait for me. "When were you gonna tell me you met our long-lost uncle from South Africa?"

"Don't you think I woulda told you if he was important?" He answers my question with a question. "How was I supposed to know the guy would follow us, with some stupid idea of a family reunion with old photographs?"

"But he's family. You didn't think to mention that we have some?" I lean on his shoulder and pull the straps back on to my heels.

"Isn't it obvious, if he's on Dad's side, he can't be on ours?"

Nearing the Lake, a few sailboats out on the water on this temperate summer day, I notice Jesse rubbing his back. "Do you think the Air Force will hire a guy with kidney problems?"

"I thought you said you were fine now." I'm royally peeved at my brother. "What else have you failed to mention?"

Jesse takes a deep breath. "For starters, Jimmy won't hire me anymore. He doesn't trust me. Fred refused to give me back my deposit. And the reason I was late was because I tried to get a job at the airport loading luggage, and they loved my suit. But who's gonna hire a guy with zero references? I'll tell you. No one. And no girl would ever wanna be with a guy like me."

I think about everything my brother just said and now it makes sense why Jesse won't give William, Billy, Uncle Billy or whatever, the time of day. He's done trusting people. And he feels spent. I get that.

"I'm sorry," I finally say. We're back at the place where we've had most of our heart-to-hearts, and I'm at a loss for words.

"You know what I think?" Jesse stops and leans over a fence railing, the murky, greenish tide of Lake Michigan hitting the cement foundation below. "I think people don't get us. And people are afraid of what they don't get."

I lean against the fence and wonder how cold the water is in the middle of the summer. But Lagan. He's different. He's the one who taught me to stop running from my fears. He can't be the only one. Silently we drift off into our own thoughts for some time, the sun rising to its peak as noon nears, my grumbling stomach reminding me I hardly touched breakfast.

"I think you shouldn't let Summer go," I say, but Jesse doesn't respond, so I keep talking. "What I mean is, she came to the hospital looking for you when she could've just forgotten about you. And she forgave you for lying about your name." Thinking about how often I kept secrets from Lagan, because I thought he couldn't handle the truth, I don't want my little brother to make the same mistake. "She seems good for you, even just as a friend."

Focused on the water, Jesse's gaze remains turned away from mine. Then like a light switch flipped on, he clasps his hands together and says, "Yeah. Sure. Maybe. But don't try and convince me I need to give our long-lost uncle a chance too. I just don't buy the whole I never knew my brother had kids all these years, and I want to be your Uncle now. He's a pawn for Dad, just like we used to be. Dad'll use him, abuse him, and ship him back to South Africa. Even if he were a halfway decent guy, which I'm not saying he is, but if he were, there's no point in getting attached when he's just gonna leave us too."

Jesse said, 'too,' and without asking, I know who he's referring to.

"Remember the time Mom took us to the beach— the time we tried to run away?" Jesse asks, his neck craned like he's straining to look beyond South Chicago to our Benton Harbor upbringing.

"Sure."

"I dream about that night too," Jesse says, "But I always change the ending."

"Me too," I say. There are a lot of endings to a lot of days I've changed in my sleep in order to find the courage to face another day.

"Well…" Jesse faces me now. "In my dreams, we always escape. But Mom, you, and I don't hitchhike our way to a new town. We swim our way across the ocean to another continent. We search for Mom's parents, find out she had a sister and we have an aunt. And her sister's married, giving us an uncle. And their kids are our cousins, and it's muddy and all of us kids play tag in the mud. And no one gets in trouble for tracking in mud. I know it's just a dream… But what threw me was I never thought to ask if Dad had any family that might want us, ya know?"

I totally know. Dad never allowed us to ask about his past or his childhood, so it just sort of disappeared with our questions. "Why do you think Dad called him? What's up Dad's sleeve?" I cringe at the irony of my words.

"So you think we should talk to him?" Jesse asks, but the tightness of his jawline suggests it would take some convincing.

"I'm not saying anything," I say, "But if you ask me, I think talking to Uncle, I mean Billy…" I stop myself, like a curse just left my lips. "Sounds so weird to call anyone Uncle, right?" I'm thinking of my time with Lagan's parents.

Jesse shrugs his shoulders, leans off the fence, then falls back on it again, the rattle of metal links startling a passing dog whose owner yanks on its leash to keep him from charging at my brother.

Once they pass us, I choose my words carefully and say, "I think it couldn't hurt to hear William's stories about Dad. It might even give us some ammunition in court. At the very least, we might learn about how he met Mom and get a little of our history."

"If this guy, what? He told you to call him Uncle Billy?" Jesse raises an eyebrow, and it's my turn to shrug. "Anyway, if our dear Uncle Billy actually tells us the truth, you have a point. He could give us valuable information that could help us with our case. Maybe Dad's mom used to pour boiling hot water on his head if he didn't finish his chores. That would explain the brain damage anyway."

A part of me wants to laugh, but I can't. It's too soon.

"So how do we find him?" I say, moving the conversation to a practical note.

Jesse pulls out his phone and says, "He texted me last week. That's why I never met with Luke. Sorry about that."

"I can't believe it!" I make Jesse stop and face me. "What if he turned out to be just like Dad? Or worse? What if Dad set him up to kidnap you or hurt you? Jesse!" I hear the sound of my risen voice and step back and wait for my breathing to steady. Speaking more calmly now, I say, "Jesse. We might not have any family, but we have each other. And if we're gonna make it through these next six months, we need each other."

Jesse nods, his eyes squinting from the sun, his arms folded over his chest falling to his side.

"Sorry," I say. "Didn't mean to go all parental lecture on you."

"I needed it." Jesse shows me his phone screen. "What should I tell him? That he might think we hate him, but we were just testing him. He passed. Now we'll have tea and crumpets with him if it so pleases him."

"Tea and crumpets?"

"I dunno. What do you think they eat in South Africa? I doubt they call it tea time there."

"Let's just ask him to meet us at the library," I say.

"Nope. That's where Summer studies."

"How 'bout the fountain?"

"That's where I blew him off the first time. With my middle finger."

"For real? Okay, then, how 'bout the Garden. It's still closed but if we stay away from the marked-off sections. Thanks to Dad, I won't get my job back, but maybe if I offer to work for free." It's worth a shot.

Jesse texts William. And almost immediately, a response pops up.

When? What time? I'll be there.

"It'll take an hour to get there on the train. And I

have to drop these heels off first or they'll have to amputate soon." My arches are killing me.

"Okay, he says, in two hours works." Jesse offers me his shoulder to lean on as we start walking back to the dorms. "Enough time to change and grab a quick lunch. Family picnic in the park it is."

And just enough time to update my Peppermint Prince.

33
~Talia~

Lagan wants me to stay. Forget the long-lost uncle, celebrate the charges being dropped, and just snuggle on the couch with him all day while he catches up with pre-semester reading. Apparently he's that student, striving to stay one step ahead of his profs. Or who just watches a Bulls game, even if it's a rerun.

"Or I could come with?" Lagan blocks my way out of his room. "Don't you think the long-lost Uncle would want to meet Dewdrop's devoted boyfriend?"

"In which case, why don't we invite Rani and Reggie too and make it a party."

"Okay." Lagan motions to Reggie, but his roomie has earbuds in while he flips through a ginormous textbook on the couch.

"I was kidding." If only he knew how much I want to be joined at the hip. But... "I just think this is something Jesse and I need to do. You understand, right?"

I ignore Lagan shaking his head and wrap my arms around his neck. When he completes the hug with his arms around my waist, Lagan gives me space to let go and move past him in the doorway. "We'll be back soon, and promise to tell you everything, okay?"

Jesse's waiting in jeans and a Chicago skyline t-shirt, and if the shirt were hunter green, we'd match. But it's silvery-grey, like the color of the El.

Looking out the train window, I watch the passing city, my brother by my side. Did you stand by your brother back in the day, Dad? When did it stop? And what made Dad's little brother show up after all this time?

Uncle Billy, even though I'm not anywhere near feeling the name yet, waits alone in the abandoned garden. Wearing a green button-down with black jeans and cowboy boots, he holds a brown bag under his arm.

"Sorry," Billy says, handing us each a plastic spoon wrapped in a napkin with an ice cream cup. "You're probably too old for me to take you out for ice cream. I guess I feel bad that I missed the window when uncles take their nieces and nephews out for hot fudge sundaes. I know I can't make up for lost time, but I…I'm really glad you both showed up today."

Jesse and I exchange looks before I say, "Thank you." Missed the window. Try growing up in a house without windows. Even before my first bite, between the color of his shirt and the vanilla ice cream gift, I feel drawn to him.

"Lekker!" Billy says, taking a spoonful of his own ice cream. When he sees the puzzled look on our faces, he translates. "Means good. Or great. We say it to describe just about anything."

Jesse walks ahead of us and dumps his unopened ice cream in the closest trash bin. I tread slowly on the gravel pathway, aware that caution tape still strings bushes to branches like garlands. Different shades of grey pepper our surroundings where once reds and golds, pinks and purples, and green, so much green, used to paint this place.

"Are you sure this is safe?" Uncle Billy asks, pointing back to the parking lot and saying, "I passed this really great park back on the train."

"This was a beautiful place once," I say, pause and then add, "There was a fire here a few months back."

"I can see that, but why would you want to meet here? Not even sure if we're supposed to be in here." Uncle Billy stops to pick up a small stone and rubs off the soot in his palm till one side of the original grey exterior reappears.

Jesse has walked so far ahead, he's out of earshot now, but my brother checks over his shoulder every few steps.

"You know your dad and I used to go to a park in Johannesburg. But Geri never liked getting dirt on his clothes. Me, I climbed the trees till all my jeans had rips in them, and just kept climbing. Geri preferred to read books in the park. He always had a book with him no matter where he went."

Wishing I had nothing in common with Dad, I focus on the part about dirt.

Uncle Billy pauses and when I don't say anything, he continues walking and talking. "One winter, I begged Mom to let us go to the park so we could play hide and seek in the dark with our classmates. She would not agree. Geri must have been in ninth grade. I was in seventh at the time, and my friends planned the game for weeks, contriving ways to trick their parents into thinking we were going to each other's houses and debating which parent was least likely to call and check on us and which parent was most likely to not answer the phone so we could come up with the perfect cover."

"Why all the trouble for a little game of hide and

143

seek?" I interject, confused. Unless South African parents are really strict and don't let their kids play hide and seek on a school night or something.

"Most South African towns had a strict curfew in place, but we were tired of being cooped up night after night." Uncle Billy pauses and smiles at me and keeps talking. "School exams were nearly over and we wanted an epic way to celebrate. So a mutual buddy of ours suggested moonless hide and seek. We waited for two nights after the full moon disappeared and met at the park with our dirt bikes before twilight to eat and then wait out the sunset."

Jesse stops and begins to walk back now, and Uncle Billy doesn't say another word until Jesse is two or three feet away from us. "Just telling your sister a story of the time your dad and I planned an adventure when we were kids."

"We can't walk much further up there. There's nowhere to go that isn't roped off." Jesse ignores Uncle Billy.

"Hold on," I say, recognizing Sergio and his buddy up the walkway. "Let me ask those guys if this one section where I used to work is any better than a couple days back." As I speed up to talk to Sergio, I glance back and see my brother looking off in a direction, facing away from Uncle Billy who appears to be rubbing something in his hand. Maybe he's still carrying that stone, but it's clear that they are not talking.

"Hi," I say, as Sergio raises his eyes and leans his rake against a fence that looks like it's been trampled on. "Any change on the willow? Is it safe to go back there yet?"

Sergio shakes his head, then adds, "Good news is the roots weren't destroyed. But if you want to see the one place that isn't ruined, the greenhouse remains sort of intact, and some of the guys have been scraping back the soot from the fireproof, glass exterior to get some sunshine to the only surviving plants in this place." Sergio must recognize the puzzle on my face. I think I remember how to get there, but I never worked that section of the garden so it's a little fuzzy. "Just back track to the parking lot and when you hit the T at the Main Offices, go left instead of right."

"Okay," I say, thanking him, heart lifted that the willow might have a fighting chance.

Joining Jesse and Uncle Billy, I direct them back to the entrance. "There's really only one place to hang out. The greenhouse is back by there to the left. Not far at all."

From the frown present on my brother's face, even one step might be too much more time spent here with our long-lost uncle. "We can always come back." Jesse shoves his hands in his jeans pockets and walks two steps ahead again, leaving me to walk next to Uncle Billy, the afternoon sun warming my face now.

"Is he always this moody?" Uncle Billy asks, with a sideways tilt of his head toward Jesse.

"Whaddya expect?" I ask, without thinking.

Uncle Billy tosses the polished stone in his hand down the pathway like he's trying to skip a rock on water, and it bounces once before skidding to a stop by the edge where dried grass resembles straw. As we pass the spot where the stone lay, I can't help but note how it doesn't fit in. Tempted to pick it up, I resist. I want to hear what happened in the rest of his story with Dad.

When we arrive at the greenhouse, the place stands out kind of like the stone, but bigger and brighter. And when I enter ahead of Jesse and Uncle Billy, both warmth and color flood my senses. Potted plants cover ledges and line the floors alongside the flowerpots spread out over tables—baby trees blooming from large planters at the bookends of each table. The glass on the exterior has tinges of black on its edges but much of it has been cleaned off, the sun making her way into this utopia preserved in a warzone.

Uncle Billy stops in front of a row of tiny purple flowers, chuckling. "African violets? Izit? Because I've never seen this back home."

"Last I heard, South Africa doesn't make up all of Africa." Jesse huffs to himself and walks further down the pathway and parks himself on a bench.

I follow him and sit next to my brother. "How much longer you gonna keep this up?" I ask. "Even if you don't like him, think you could keep your snide comments to yourself long enough for me to learn something about Dad?"

Jesse shrugs his shoulder and says, "Fine," and juts out his jaw and leans back, arms crossed.

Uncle Billy walks up and sits opposite us on a separate bench, looking at his phone. "You're correct. African violets grow in Eastern Africa, where the climate and temperatures create the perfect condition for them to blossom. Shame. If these beauties grew in my backyard, I'd pick them every day for my girlfriend."

So he's not married. Hmm. I guess that probably means no cousins that we don't know of.

Jesse wears a smug look on his face. I guess it didn't hurt that he was "right" about the violets. I'm just glad he's keeping his mouth shut for now.

"So what happened when you and Dad played hide and seek back in that story?" I ask, anxious to hear the outcome.

"Oh that. Yes," Uncle Billy says, eyeing Jesse whose attention appears to be off watching a bee buzz up above. "Where was I? So about ten of us agreed to meet

at the park with snacks and fuel up before it got dark, all
with alibis we felt would hold strong until the next
morning. Ag Geri, he didn't want to do it, but I
convinced him that if he didn't, the guys would think he
was a wimp, so he finally gave in and joined me, but he
insisted we walk, because he didn't want to ride his bike
back in the dark. Which of course made us arrive last to
the designated spot in the park. By the time we joined
our crew, everyone was ready to play, making us an easy
target. I shoved my snacks into Geri's arms, announcing,
'You're it!' and took off running with the others."

My eyes grew wide as I imagined a shorter, younger
version of Dad left alone in the shadow of a playground
slide towering over him.

"Geri stood there, arms full of biscuits, mangos and
beef rolls, left to count, but no one told him the
boundaries, how long to count or what was base." Uncle
Billy leans forward on his bench. "Geri was older. I felt
no need to worry, and looked at it as a chance for my
big brother to make his mark and maybe even break the
wimp status he'd acquired over the years. He usually
passed on the guy stunts we all jumped at for a chance
to be part of. The guys weren't stupid. He said he had
homework one too many times, but as I ran to hide in
the pitch black with my best friend Joseph, I rooted for
my big brother to be crowned Game Warrior that night.
Only if you captured every person in hiding would you
earn that badge, and only two of the fellows claimed that
fame—Mickey and Berns."

"What kind of name is Berns?" I can't help but ask.

"Berns. Short for Bernard?"

Right. Of course.

"Anyway," Uncle Billy says. "While the rest of us
hid, Mickey and Berns decided to play a gag on Geri.
When he finished counting and announced, 'Ready or

not, here I come,' the two followed him from a distance so Geri couldn't see them. But as Geri inched his way around the park, bumping into equipment, Mickey and Burns took turns tossing rocks at him, which startled Geri, but from what they said, he kept looking. Then they took long branches and started poking him in the back. But instead of turning, grabbing the sticks and figuring out who was following him, Geri took off running in the opposite direction. After waiting it out awhile behind trees in the adjoining forest, Joseph thought Geri gave up and we won, joking quietly how great he'd look in his invisible warrior crown when he had his turn to be seeker. Only when I snuck my way back to the big slide, did I realize Joseph had run off. I thought he was joking when he said he'd find a new hiding place and stay there till the sunrise if that's how long it took to keep the crown from Geri. Alone, I tried to hide behind the slide at the other end of playground, but I could see some of the other guys in the open. They had given up on Geri coming to find them. And the game. Maybe we'd start a new round. Meanwhile, some neighbors must have started a bonfire, I thought, because I remember smelling smoke and thinking of roasted marshmallows, wishing I had snagged some snacks before leaving Geri. But just as I debated how much longer I should stay hiding, the wooden playground structure went up in flames and Geri ran around saying, "Gotcha. Found you. Found you too," till the entire group was caught and he won the game. Everyone except for Joseph."

"So you're saying that Dad was a pyromaniac long before he ever came to America?" Jesse asks the question, and I hit him in the arm, afraid his sarcasm might end the story.

But Uncle Billy continues. "I'm not sure, because no

one stuck around to find out who set the fire. By the time the cops showed up, we all fled and ran back home, each of us taking a licking from our folks for lying but it seemed like a better option than spending the night in jail. Geri offered his back to Dad's belt first. I went second and as we lay in bed that night, Geri confessed to starting the fire, a certain pride in his voice noticeable even in the dark."

"Did you tell anyone?" I asked, afraid of what Billy would say next. I look over and Jesse's sitting on the edge of his seat now, too.

"Geri told me he'd set my bed on fire while I slept if I ever told a soul. And the crazy thing is that no one ever found out. The morning news reports blamed it on vigilante Kaffirs, and Geri got away with murder that night."

"What's a Kaffir? And don't you mean arson?" I ask.

"Kaffir is the word we Dutch South Afrikaners use for the dark-skinned South Africans. And no, I did not mean arson. What happened to Joseph is still a mystery but my best guess is that he refused to be found by Geri and stayed hidden. The fire ate up the grounds so fast, it's a wonder the rest of us escaped only smelling like smoke. Joseph—"Billy's voice cracks. "Joey didn't get so lucky. After firefighters put out the flames, they found his fourteen-year-old body, barbecued to a crisp. If it weren't for his braces, his body... let's just say, they knew it was him."

Nausea rises in my throat as Uncle Billy continues his story. "No one came forward the next day. Not one of us. We just let Joey's parents live in denial for nearly a week, believing he was missing. Then the dental reports finally came in, confirming his identity, but his mother went nuts. Coming by our house, demanding answers, because, she claimed, her son didn't even know how to light a match. He did. I'd lit plenty of matches with Joey. But you don't mention that when you're face to face with an angry, mourning, mom. And Geri. He stayed silent. Never said a word about Joey's death after that first night. But believe me, the guys never teased him again. Ever. He earned a different crown that night. One I get the feeling he never took off."

We sit in silence for a bit, digesting in our own way. Jesse speaks up first, his arms crossed again. "So what are you really doing here?"

"Geri asked me to come. He needed my help." Uncle Billy sounds genuinely concerned for Dad as I search for signs of theatrics.

"But why now? Why bother after all these years?" Jesse wants more. I agree.

"Can I tell you about the last time I saw Geri first? The last time any of us saw him, twenty-five years ago?" Uncle Billy looks back and forth between Jesse and me.

Jesse shrugs his shoulders.

"So Geri went on to read his books, always ranking top in his class, and no one ever made fun of him again, but no one liked him either. Then high school graduation drew near and prom, and everyone paired off but Geri remained dateless, until one day, a girl asked him to prom. She transferred in sophomore year and kept to her books, so no one really knew her. Her name was Shanti and she was, I don't know if teens still use this term, but 'nerdy' and dark-skinned."

"Wait, what?" Jesse says.

"Isn't Shanti an Indian name? Was she from India?" I ask.

"From a few generations back," Uncle Billy says, "But with Mandela's release, more non-Dutch students trickled into our school district. Most of us had no room for them. The country was changing, but we weren't ready for change if that makes sense. We were young. Ignorant. Just weren't brought up to think all races were equal. You hear any lie long enough, you start to believe it."

"Then what happened?" Jesse asks, his body leaning forward on the bench again.

"Shanti showed up at the house on Prom night, no glasses, hair down, wearing a dress all the girls would envy, but my mother took one look at the color of her skin and ushered her out, telling her, 'There's been a mistake, honey. You must have the wrong address.' I saw the whole thing happen and just watched her leave and then rather enjoyed Geri's shock when he came down the stairs to find his date gone. He cursed out Mother and ran after her, and I guess he must have caught up with her, but he didn't come home that night. And when he did, no one said a word. Like prom never happened, everyone returned to their routines, but it was understood, Shanti wasn't welcome in our home, and Geri snuck out every night to meet her. I'd hear about it the next day in school. 'Saw your brother making out with the brown princess in the library.' Or at the movies. Or at the ice cream parlor in town, off in a corner booth. Shameless."

"Greenhouse's locking up in about fifteen minutes, folks," a security guard tells us. "Sorry."

"No. We understand. We'll be done in a minute," I say, waiting for her to walk off and then turn to Uncle Billy. "Go on."

"A month before graduation, Shanti's parents show up with the police. They want to arrest Geri for making their daughter pregnant. They claim he raped her. If I thought Mother was upset before, Father went through the roof. Geri wasn't home from school yet, but I knew he was probably off with Shanti somewhere. The cops and parents settled into our living room and we all waited. And waited.

"Around midnight, Geri finally showed up, smelling of cigarette smoke and rum, and the cops were in the process of cuffing him when he blurts out, 'I want proof. Are there any witnesses? You can't arrest me without some evidence.'

"And the crazy thing is, he was right. Shanti's parents were trying to end the secret relationship they had just discovered, but they had no idea who they were dealing with. Geri packed his bags that night and told us he was leaving for America with Shanti, and Father told him, 'I won't leave you one red hot cent if you walk out that door.' Geri didn't look back when he left. Never hugged any of us. Just left like that. Not even a year later, Shanti returned to South Africa, begged her parents to forgive her, and the last I heard, she was never pregnant by Geri, but her parents moved with her back to India and married her off there to someone from their ethnicity."

"So she came back. What about Dad?" I ask, keenly aware of the now setting sun moving down the glass structure that surrounds us.

"He never came back. In fact, the few times our parents were able to track him down, he refused to communicate with them, no explanation. On Dad's deathbed, he even offered to reverse his will and reinstate Geri's portion of the inheritance, but he never answered any of our calls or letters or emails. We honestly had no idea he had married, had kids, or anything."

"So your dad is gone? How about your mom?" Jesse's asking.

"Both died last year. I'm the last one, and when I got the call from Geri two weeks ago that he was in trouble, I just came. I didn't ask why. And that's why I'm here."

The female security guard stands by the greenhouse exit now, door propped open. It's time to go. And as we leave, I'm thinking of a girl who might have loved Dad, but not enough to stay with him. Parents who rejected Dad, but regretted their anger and reached out to him again without success. And Dad. He was all alone. Just like now.

34
~Talia~

As we leave, the three of us walk silently through Glenco back to the train. Jesse no longer walks ahead but keeps in step with us. And the gap between him and Uncle Billy seems narrowed. Just a little.

As I steal glances at Uncle Billy and think of Dad, I wonder if some people just never move past their pain. Like quick sand, they're just trapped, their minds stuck in the muck of all life's punches?

At the station, Uncle Billy says, "To be honest, I felt relieved when Geri took off, because his presence reminded me of the fire and Joey, and I can honestly say that it took years before I forgave him."

"Why?" Jesse stops himself, and rephrases. "How did you decide you could forgive him?"

The train comes to a screeching stop and the doors slide open in front of us. "That's a story for another day, son," Billy reaches out and touches Jesse's shoulder, and he shakes it off, moving a single seat away from me and Uncle Billy. "Just know forgiving doesn't mean you ever forget."

I sit next to Billy. "Sorry."

"You never have to say sorry for someone else. Everyone has their reasons. And each person makes their own choices."

Until our stop, no one speaks, although a thousand more questions rage inside of me. But one shouts the loudest, and it makes no sense to ask it so early in this relationship, but it burns inside me like a kid who can't wait till her birthday to tear open her presents. I don't know that experience, but I know that I was supposed to know it.

And now, our uncle, by blood, a man who might have spent time with us if he had known we existed shows up. As childish as the question may sound, it's been playing on repeat ever since he handed over the ice cream. I'm dying to ask him, "Now that you've met us, do you want us?"

But I can't chance the answer being no. I don't know what I'd do if he said no.

Being with the ladies at Hope Now awakened a thirst in me. Cooking together, living together, sharing one another's stories. Even though I knew it was transient, I wanted more. I wanted to feel like that more often. Like I belonged. Like I had a place where I fit, and things made sense.

Spending those few hours with Lagan's parents, I saw how it works. Family. Little things, like Lagan watching the game with his dad. His mom brushing rice off his dad's chin. Moments of habit, endearment, and tradition. From hunger to craving, I want it more than I've ever allowed myself to.

And here comes this man, a complete stranger, but by birth, he's part of us, and with each story he shares, I want to trust him. I want to believe that he's wants to trust us too. To let us in.

We're three stops from where Jesse and I get off. "I

was wondering," I say to Billy, trying to keep my voice low so Jesse can't hear. "Will we see you again? How long are you staying in Chicago for?"

Uncle Billy sighs. "My flight leaves in a few days. I have to get back to the business."

Like a hot air balloon whisked away before I ever had the chance to board, I want to kick myself for getting my hopes up.

"But I was talking to Geri, and he's considering helping me run the show once this whole trial blows over."

You're going to help him? He averts my glare and shifts in his seat.

Doesn't he even read the papers on what the reporters are calling Dad? Counselor Gerard Vanderbilt: An Epic Charlatan Burn Warden and A Champion of Human Trafficking—*Yes, one of the Bad Guys.*

"Maybe my family's to blame for what happened to Geri." Bill rubs the top of one hand and then switches and rubs the top of the other, like he's trying to remove an invisible layer of dirt. "Maybe if we hadn't cut him off, maybe he'd have returned home too and none of this. All these mistakes and misunderstandings. I can't say for sure, but I wonder if things would have turned out differently if our father hadn't been so harsh."

My face feels hot with anger. "I don't get it." I say out loud. "Didn't you just say that each person makes their own choices?" He can't just write off all the wrong Dad did with the excuse that his family rejected him.

One stop remains before Jess and I have to get off the train, and like I have an allergic reaction, I can't sit so close to this man I thought wanted to get to know his newfound family. I don't even know if I want him to be my family after what he just said. Rising to my feet, I stumble my way to the exit, facing forward so I won't have to face my disappointment.

"Can we meet in the morning for breakfast before my flight?" Uncle Billy says from behind me, but I pretend I don't hear him as the train comes to a stop. "Text me," Bill adds when the doors part and the announcement overhead says, "Union Station. Stand clear of the closing doors," and I get off, Jesse on my heels.

I don't say goodbye. Out of the corner of my eye, I can see Uncle Billy raising his hand to wave, then lowering it. Jesse and I walk down to the sidewalk in silence and instead of going straight to the dorms, I feel the Lake calling me. I need some time to think about what happened today.

"I'll meet you back up at Lagan's place in a bit. Just need some air," I say, but Jesse stops in his tracks.

"It sucks, doesn't it?" He's not really asking.

I fight back tears, wanting to hide behind sunglasses, but the sun's almost gone. Street lamps flicker and neon store fronts blaze bright all around, nudging me toward shadows. I know the last time I went off on my own, Dad found me, threatened me, and it got ugly. And I know he's out there, but the restraining order is in effect now, and the bottom line is, he'll always be out there, somewhere, until he dies. Pushing my fear to the edge has been like clearing a smooth place on the beach to build a sandcastle. No matter how much I clear, sand is all I have. So I either give up or learn to make something with it. Tonight, I want to build a castle out of stars.

"I'll come with." Jess steps forward. "Just to bother you. You know, in case you slip off the rocks and fall in. I'll be there to text 911 so someone who knows how to swim will know where to find you."

I can't say no to my little brother, not when he's

been through just as much as me. Maybe more.

"For the record," Jesse says, as we turn the corner and walk down Monroe Street. "I knew he was a chump. I mean, if you really want to make up for lost time, buy me a Porsche, bay-bee. I want something that ain't gonna melt."

"Or a diamond necklace," I say, following the chain on my neckline till the blue glass heart lies between my fingers. "So I can pawn it and pay off some college tuition."

As we walk down to the Lake we bump shoulders and add to our wish list. Pony rides. Jet planes. Long gowns. And speedboats.

The phone buzzes, making Jesse stop. He reads the text out loud.

"I delayed my departure for a few weeks. Found someone to cover the business. Can we meet again? I've shared some stories. But I want to hear some from you."

Before I protest, another text rolls in and he reads that one too. "Jesse, sorry for eavesdropping the other day, but I found a flight school north of Chicago. Can I sign you up for a few lessons? Consider them a belated birthday present. I'll text you the details, and maybe I can come and watch."

Jesse looks at me. Then back to the phone. "I know what he's trying to do."

"Does it matter what he's trying to do?" I say.

Smiling, Jesse messages, I'll take the lessons minus the company.

There's a pause and then the reply comes in. Okay. Will message you tomorrow with details. Can we still meet and talk with your sister though?

This time I take the phone from my brother, type, Will there be ice cream? and hand it back.

He laughs out loud. "Good one."

The response reads: Burgers too. If you like. Let me know when.

Jess types, We'll let you know.

Putting the phone away, Jesse says, "I'll bet he needs time to talk to Dad. And if he has half a brain, he'll see through Dad's lies. But who knows? And who cares? I never promised that we'd meet up with him."

At the lake, the moonlight sparkles on the water, like stars dancing on the waves. A short distance from the city lights, a handful of the brightest stars dot the orange-black sky, and as I connect them, they make a pot with a handle. May as well be a teapot. Dad's so-called choices burn me—even here.

Rubbing my arms over my sleeves, I tell Jesse, "Let's go."

"But we just got here."

"I'm cold."

"Fine, let's go, but see that blinking star up there? The one moving smoothly across the sky?"

I see it.

"Someday, that's gonna be me... soaring through stars." Jesse's eyes follow the blinking light as it moves across the sky, his neck craned toward the sky. "And I'm gonna take you with me. Yes, I am."

35
~Talia~

Reggie's head lies on top of an open text on the table, the TV blaring the ten o'clock news. Jesse retrieves the remote, plops down on a couch, and starts flipping channels. Passing the lounge, I reach up to knock on Lagan's open door, but stop a moment and just stare at my Peppermint Prince, his back to me. He's doing pull-ups, hanging off his loft ridge, his knees bent to keep his feet from brushing the carpet below.

"Do you always spy on people when they're working out?" Lagan says, finishing another pull-up before landing on his feet. His smile lights up as he approaches me in the doorway. "How was your time with the new uncle, Dewdrop?"

I don't know how to answer the question, but I'm happy to move into his open arms, and just lay my head on Lagan's chest.

"That good, huh?" he asks.

After a short recap of the time with Billy, Lagan grabs a pair of sweatpants from the back hooks on the door. "Get some sleep, Dewdrop. Had plans to take a walk, but we'll catch those falling stars another night.

See you in my dreams." And he makes the motion like he's taking a basketball shot toward me before leaving me alone in his room.

Climbing up to sleep under my Post-it covered sky, I lie back on Lagan's loft and peel off my jeans, pushing them off to the side of me, and nestle into the pillow.

In my dreams, I'm following the woman in the garden one more time. She finally caught up to the gardener. This time, there are also three people walking on a journey, each carrying something, but they only travel at night, their only guide the stars. One particular star.

"What are they doing?" the woman asks the gardener.

"They move toward a promise," he says.

I look between the travelers and the woman, but they can't see me.

"They've been walking for days. Months. What do they hope to find?" the woman asks the gardener.

"Me."

"But why at night? And what about the cloudy nights. What about when they're too tired to keep walking. What about the times when all they see is darkness?"

"It's in our darkest hour when we need hope. And searching for it, believing you'll find it, not giving up— that's what changes you."

The woman's not done with her questions. "What about when they arrive? How will they know it's you?"

This time the gardener doesn't answer. Not with words, anyway. Instead he just opens up his hands. And the woman nods, tears slipping down her cheeks. Because his hands are scarred. His palms are a mirror. She's not alone.

36
~Jesse~

Before walking into Lagan's dorm room to grab a few things the next morning, I peek at the phone. As promised, Uncle Billy messaged an address and phone number to the flight school with a note to call and schedule a lesson. Today's to-do list includes: hunt for a job, give Lagan some money, and learn to fly.

Lagan greets me with, "I never knew you were into flying?"

Talia must have told him about the Air Force dream. Shrugging, I walk over and sift through my life's belongings for some cash and fresh clothes for the day.

"So?" Talia says, rustling my hair. "Might have to get you a bigger helmet if your hair keeps growing though."

"Riding a plane's not like riding a bike," I say, rolling my eyes at my sister. "Pilots don't wear helmets unless they're flying in war. I think."

"I'd wear one if I knew the guy behind the steering wheel had never flown before." Lagan cocks his head sideways and adds, "Just sayin'."

"So did he text about the lessons? Did you call?" Talia asks. "Maybe we can come out and watch?"

I shake my head. I sure as heck don't want anyone to see me screw up on my first try. "I'll pass on having fans in the stands, but can I thank you for letting us crash here? We're gonna work something out soon. A place for Talia and me." I pull out some bills from the sock.

"How about you pay me back someday with a flight over Lake Michigan." Lagan says, shaking his head. "That would be su-weet. But just so you know, you don't have to rush out of here. The couch is kinda comfy. And the company's not half bad either." Lagan flashes Talia a smile, moving toward her, my cue to jet.

Sure. I'll fly you anywhere after I take Dad on a one-way flight to the moon and drop him off. Without a cell phone. The invitation also reminds me of Summer and churros. And a request for purple roses from Paris which makes two flights I owe now. I don't know when I'll be able to pay up, but I do know that someone's paying for the groceries and the phone bill. Not to mention the money he gave me when I first took off on my own.

"Here's a hundred," I say, putting five twenties on top of the dresser. "Just take it. I'll pay you more when I get a new job. I promise."

"You really don't have to."

I shut the door behind me, escaping his hand trying to return the cash.

"Hey," Talia catches me in the hallway by the arm before I head to the showers. "Just check in when we're not together to let me know you're okay. For me."

"You don't have to worry about me."

"But I do. I always will," Talia says, looking me in the eyes.

I throw a glance in the direction of Lagan. "Sure, I adore him, but you're all I got."

I swallow hard. She's totally right. I just... I want her to be free. Go live her life with Lagan. Stop thinking about me. A few steps past the couches toward the windows in the suite and Talia follows me.

"What now?" I ask.

"What's wrong?" She asks, and I don't answer as I stare out the tall windows overlooking Lake Michigan. Waves ride toward shore, crash against the rocks, and then recede again, leaving a white bubbly residue that fizzles, and then the whole scene repeats.

"Is it Lagan?" Talia asks when I don't say anything. "Cuz he's just trying to help."

"You can tell him I'm good." Maybe I answer too quickly. But maybe he needs to stick to being there for Talia.

Talia's hand slips off my shoulder as I walk away, but not before I hear her last words. "Everyone needs help sometimes."

37
~Jesse~

The phone rings three times and goes into voicemail.
Maybe everyone's busy flying planes and can't answer
the phone. Not sure if the same rules apply as driving a
car, but maybe it's dangerous to talk and fly at the same
time. In either case, I'll call back after I check out some
jobs. Or leave a message. Or call back. Or—

"Uh…Yes. My name's John, I mean Jesse. Actually,
Justice Vanderbilt. And I wanted to—"

"Hello? Can you hold for a second?" A live voice
comes on but doesn't wait for me to say yes.

I'm on hold. As the El rumbles by overhead, I kick
myself for having a name crisis.

"Your name?" The voice is back. It's a woman.

"Justice Vanderbilt. I wanted to schedule a flying
lesson." I'm pleased with myself for not stuttering.

"Right. Someone called this morning. Your first
three lessons are covered. Now just a few logistics. Are
you over eighteen?"

So Uncle Billy seems to be a man of his word. "Yes,
I'm eighteen."

"Great. Bring proof. Have any heart issues or other

health issues that will interfere with your ability to function at optimum conditions?"

"No." I rub the back of my right side.

"Any issues with heights?"

"Nope." Not that I know of, anyway.

"Alrighty then. We can get you in some time in November."

"November? That's, like, what? Four or five months away!"

"Hold on."

Waiting again, I work on calming myself down, ducking into a coffee shop to avoid another loud rumbling from another train. I've waited eighteen years to figure out I even have a dream, so what's a few months more? I'll apologize when the woman gets back on the phone. Piano music plays on the phone as I wait.

"Are you free this afternoon? Someone just called in to cancel. It happens sometimes. You got lucky."

I'm holding my breath. If I say yes...

"Justice? Are you still there? Look. I have to get ready for the next class. The session starts at three in the afternoon. If you want it, say the word or else I'll give it to the next person who calls. Hold on. There's another call—"

"I'll take it." I say, exhaling into the receiver. "I'll see you at three."

"Come fifteen minutes early." The phone clicks and the call is over.

Stepping outside to the clear blue skies, I'm thankful for great flying conditions.

The school is located in the Northwest suburbs of Chicago, and I just have one stop first. Calling the hospital Social Work department, I find out that yes, in fact, they did receive my new I.D.

"Will you be coming by to pick it up soon?"

"I'm around the corner." I am. Pretty much.

"And how are you feeling, Jesse?" And that's when I recognize the voice of Ms. Dillon, the crisis worker. "Dr. Singh wants to know if you've scheduled your follow-up?"

"Umm…" I conveniently forgot. "I'll call and make an appointment." I press End and walk a few blocks over.

The hospital security gives me a visitor badge, and I hit the elevator button for the sixth floor, but the shaft stops at the fourth floor, and a nurse backs up with a patient in a wheelchair.

"Nurse Sheela?" I recognize her before she turns to face me.

"Jesse?" She lets go of the handle bars of the wheelchair and holds my shoulders. "How you holding up? You came back to say a proper goodbye, son?"

The elevator dings and opens. It's my stop. I move around Nurse Sheela, but not before saying, "Thank you. For taking care of me when I was here."

She nods and lets out a "Mmm-hmm," but she's not smiling. As the elevator doors close, a twinge of guilt rises inside me, because Nurse Sheela did more than take care of me. She made me feel like I mattered—with cake. And the application for a new I.D. was her idea.

The office manager in Social Work hands over my new government I.D. after making me sign for it. Checking the time, I remind myself that I have to arrive early to the flight school or chance waiting five months before I fly a plane.

As I exit the hospital, I feel a tad queasy. Realizing I haven't eaten, I jump on the Blue line going out toward the flight school in Wheeling, vowing to pick up something to munch on before I sign in for my lesson.

Checking the phone, I see Talia didn't text me.

167

Instead of texting her to let her know I'm having my
first lesson, I google tips for first-time flying and get lost
in link after link, each emphasizing something different.

As I scroll down, the announcer overhead says,
"O'Hare Airport. Last stop." So focused on the details I
can't memorize fast enough, only when the conductor
walks by collecting all the items passengers forgot on the
train do I realize the train has stopped moving.

"Need an umbrella?" he says, holding three out to
me, but then sticks them in the large black garbage bag
he's towing. "Kidding. But you'd think on a day like
today, riders would make sure they don't walk off the
train without theirs."

What? Rain? As I exit the train and follow the signs
for the bus terminal, my eyes are glued skyward. Clouds
roll in, the sun only half as bright as it was this morning.
Dialing the flight school, I wait one ring, two, and then
on the third, someone picks up—this time a man.

"Nope," he answers my question. "We don't cancel
lessons because of weather."

"Not even if a tornado's coming through?" I ask.
Maybe I need to rethink the risks verses the benefits of
this flying dream.

"There's no tornado in today's forecast, if you're
worried."

"Umm. Okay." My gaze hasn't left the sky where
more grey clouds hide the sun. "Thanks."

Bus number 209 drops me about a mile from the
small, private airport, and as I walk the final distance, a
hundred times I consider turning around. What's
another few months in the grand scheme of things? But
my feet propel me forward even if I left my courage on
the train with the abandoned umbrellas. Resorting to
self-talk, I remind myself, at least it's not raining.

And then I feel it. A drop of water on my forehead.

And then one on my nose. But by the time I arrive at the front door of Jet Green's Flight School, the rain ceases and the clouds seem to be clearing too. Relieved, and a glance at the phone tells me I am just on time, but not early.

As I wait for a big guy to finish talking to the woman behind the counter, I scan the room. There are model airplanes hanging from the ceiling, and on all the walls, wallpaper of the Wright Brothers and their historical flight depicted in various stages. From scenes of the siblings building the plane to painting the plane. To testing the plane. And on the final wall, landing the plane. Above that last wall, the quote, "Any landing you can walk away from is a good one!" — Gerald R. Massie, U.S. Army Air Forces photographer captions the photograph of the brothers next to their plane on solid ground.

"You're late," the woman behind the counter wearing a Cubs hat over her short black hair catches my attention. "Justice, correct?"

I clear my throat and say, "I'm sorry, I took a train and a bus…"

"Save it." She pushes papers over to me. "Fill this out during the introduction that's starting in…" She looks at her wrist watch. "Two minutes. And sign everything and give it back to me before you go out onto the tarmac. I'll check your ID and everything else before you board any plane, okay?"

"Can I borrow a pen, Laura? Please?" Her name tag reads, Laura Kim.

She takes one from a mug on the counter and says, "You can have this one if you call me, 'Oh Captain, my Captain.'"

"Oh—"

"I was kidding," she says, her scowl relaxed to a

smile now. "You're gonna be a fun one to teach. Now go on. And get here early next time."

Right. I knew she was joking, I tell myself. I at least suspected it. And as I turn to find an empty seat to fill out my application, she says, "Wait, one more thing? When's the last time you ate?"

I didn't. And like a sleepy giant that didn't know he was sleeping until he was stirred awake, my stomach makes a low grumble. "A while ago." A long while.

"The newbies always think they need to fly on empty, because they're afraid they'll be nervous and puke while three thousand feet up. But it's better to be a little queasy than to be light-headed from hunger. That's when you can't think straight. And you know what good ol' Bevo said."

I shake my head, and she walks over, points out a bowl of fruit for the taking on the end table and pats the top of my clipboard. The quote across the top sheet reads, "Remember. You fly an airplane with your head. Not your hands and feet." –Bevo Howard.

Scarfing down a banana, I scroll down the application to the easy part. The health report and I check no for all the questions about medical history, although I feel a tad guilty for not saying yes when it comes to the question of mental illness in the family. Do Mom's two nervous breakdowns count? Since she was never officially diagnosed, I flip the page and keep checking.

"Done." I hand the clipboard back to Laura.

She scans each page and then says, "Two blanks. You have to fill all the emergency contacts in."

But I already included Lagan's number.

Laura says, "Just put in a neighbor. A friend. Your pet." She waits a beat, then says, "Kidding. Pets do not count."

SOARING THROUGH STARS

Looking at my cell phone, I scrawl two names, one
after the other, and pen in the phone numbers from the
contacts' page, and Laura takes the sheet and directs me
to a computer monitor and hands me a pair of
headphones in a plastic bag. I unwrap them and push
the buds in my ears, she hits play, and the Introduction
to Flying film starts.

Glancing out the windows, I'm thrilled to see the sun
shining brightly again. Blue skies, here I come.

38
~Jesse~

The video on flying lasts twenty minutes, and I
recognize many terms from the Google searches I
skimmed on the train. And when the credits roll, Laura
flips the monitor off and holds out a set of keys to me.
"Ready to take the wheel?"

Uh? N to the O. When I don't reach for the keys,
Laura starts laughing, hangs her hat on a nearby
coatrack, revealing a few grey strands streaked through
her black head of hair. "If I let anyone walk in here and
take one of my babies and fly solo on the first day, I'd
be a bad parent. We all need to hold someone's hand
when we start out. So let's hop to it." And she hands me
a logbook, pulls her shades over her black eyes, and
walks outdoors.

I follow Laura over to the white Cessna 172. If it
were a little bigger, wouldn't it be safer?

When Laura opens the driver's seat door and says,
"After you?" I climb aboard and put on my seatbelt
while she circles around to the passenger seat, and
assures me just like the video described, "This is a co-
piloted plane. There are many reasons pilots rarely fly

solo. Team effort, double the vision up there, and honestly, to keep each other awake on long flights." She laughs. I don't. But I clasp my hands together when I notice them shaking.

"Okay." Laura points to two gadgets on the panel in front of us. "First step to pre-flight check is to make sure the readings match up with the log book." And they do.

Laura patiently shows me all of the instruments, then walks me through a pre-flight inspection around the outside of the plane. I learn about Hobbs meters and flaps, how to communicate with Air Traffic Control, how to untie the plane, and a million other things.

We exit the plane, and sample the fuel from the left wing, and once the walk-around finishes, Laura says, "We're all clear. Looking good." Laura pats the side of the plane like a friend, and I feel more relaxed now that we've spent so much time going over details. I also feel my heart racing as I enter the plane again.

With only fifteen minutes left on the clock of my lesson, Laura says, "We have time to do a few patterns, okay." Patterns mean repeated landings around the airport with very little time to fly too high. I'm in.

Laura points to the taxi line and says, "Let's rev her up and slowly make our way over to the starting line," and when the plane rumbles with the start of the engine, my heart pounds even faster. Looking all around to make sure nothing is within any nearness for crashing into unless I go in reverse a few hundred feet, I ease my foot off the brakes and engage the accelerator just like the video instructed.

Coming to a jarring stop a few feet from the taxi line, Laura clears her throat and says, "A little further. Just a little. And now that you feel how sensitive the brakes are, you can practice a little gentler push when we get to the line." And I do, and Laura nods, pleased with the minor change.

"Now, you can read this script to ATC, and we wait for the green light to take off."

I look around, but no physical traffic light exists out here. And then I read, "Chicago-Ground, this is Cessna N82745U at the South Ramp, requesting taxi for takeoff, remaining in the pattern."

A voice comes on and says, "Cessna 25 Uniform, taxi from Alpha to runway 21."

Twenty-one—meaning 210 degrees... "There?" I point to where I think runway 21 would be, and Laura lifts her sunglasses, smiles and nods, and pulls her shades back down.

Deep breath as I approach the runway, and my heart pounds, possibly more strongly than I can ever recall, and I rub my chest downward, but the blue skies start to turn lighter blue. Like the color of a light blue crayon. And the sky transforms into my little boy picture. The one I brought home to my dad of my airplane named N.E.Where. The one he called messy, crumpled up, and threw away.

If you could see me now, Dad?

As I make my way over to the runway, I do a run-up, just as the video instructed, making sure the airplane sounds okay and seems to be in top working condition. Then I make my way over to the hold short line beside the runway.

There I read the next script Laura points to over the mouthpiece to ATC. "Chicago tower, C25U holding short at runway 21, ready for takeoff, remaining in the pattern."

And the Tower responds, "C25U, clear for takeoff, make right traffic, and report midfield at the downwind."

Turning to Laura, I cover my mouthpiece and say, "So, I should turn right when in the air and at the end of the runway?" and she nods yes, and maybe I imagine it, but when she puts her clipboard to her side, she seems to lean back in her chair and relax.

Which makes me all the more aware of my beating heart that pounds like it means to break out of my chest now. Massaging my chest some more, I look around for a bottle of water, but there isn't one in sight.

"Ready when you are," Laura says, eyes straight ahead.

My hands feel clammy as I rub my forehead to try and clear up the hazy feeling, but it only grows stronger.

"I... I ..." Feel dizzy. "I can't," I say out loud.

I need to sit down. Problem is, I am already sitting, and it doesn't help.

39
~Jesse~

When I come to, the plane is taxiing back to its parking spot, but my hands aren't on the steering wheel. *Is it over?*

"Don't feel bad." Laura's directing the Cessna from her side of controls. "You're not the first to get nervous and blank out right before takeoff."

"No!" I shake my head and think back to the last thing I remembered, and curse Dad under my breath. He's the last thing I was thinking about. "I feel so stupid...But I wasn't nervous." Maybe I started nervous, but when ATC gave us the go ahead for takeoff, I was ready.

"Sure. Fine. You forgot to mention you're allergic to bananas, then." Laura smiles, and I guess I should be relieved that she's not mad or annoyed for the time I wasted. "We'll go with that. But just so you know, I radioed ahead and the office made a call to your emergency contact."

What? "You're kidding me! But I'm fine. I feel. Fine."

"Don't take it personally. It's a liability thing." Laura

pats my steering wheel. "Help me park this puppy, but I won't disengage my side of the controls. And understand that we just have a legal obligation to our students to make sure they don't leave the property alone if they have an episode."

I'm shaking my head, annoyed that my sister and probably Lagan will be waiting for me back there.

"Look on the bright side," Laura says as she presses the brakes, perfectly. "At least you passed out for less than thirty seconds. Any longer and we would have been obligated to call an ambulance, but you came to, and once our on-site health official checks your vitals, you're free to leave. Accompanied by someone, of course."

I'm kicking myself as I glance up at the still blue skies, wanting to curse them too from not letting me get a little closer.

"One more tiny detail, my friend," Laura says, retrieving the log book and documenting the changes in the gauges. "Before we try again, you'll need medical clearance in the event that what happened back there was a health issue and not a case of first flight jitters. And try to keep from getting your doctor uncle to make one up. We can read, and same last names never fly." Laura raises an eyebrow. "Pun intended."

Laura's kind enough to let me follow her through the post-flight routine, and after every couple of items, she nods in my direction, reassuring me we'll do this again. Shuffling back to the main building, I pull out my phone, but there are surprisingly no messages from Talia or Lagan. There is one from—

"Jesse!" I hear Summer's voice before I finish reading her text. "Are you okay? Is everything okay?" She's wearing a blue sweater—blue like her eyes—over a grey skirt. Grey like how I feel inside now that she probably knows I failed to take off.

Looking away and then back down at the phone, Summer spoke the words of her text. Two questions. One answer.

"I'm fine." I say and walk slightly ahead of her. And even though I'm clearly not in the mood to talk, Summer stands next to me, and asks, "Maybe you were just a little nervous. Or it had something to do with your kidneys?"

I shake my head, because I'm not answering that question, but the gentleman approaching, wearing a stethoscope and glancing over some papers says, "What's wrong with your kidneys? You never mentioned any kidney problems on the application."

I glare at Summer, but I'm more angry at myself for putting her name down on the emergency contact list. "I had acute renal failure," I blurt out, because there's no point in lying now. "But that was a few weeks ago. I'm fine now."

"Did you consume any items high in potassium before the flight?" the doc, I think he's a doctor, asks.

"A banana," Laura answers. "It's my fault. I showed him the fruit bowl, but I assumed he knew what he could and couldn't eat."

I feel even more stupid now. Duh. Bananas. Potassium. Dr. Singh warned me about keeping away from it for the next little while.

"I got here as fast as I could," a man with a strong accent says from behind us, a South African accent.

As if I didn't already feel two inches tall, Uncle Billy rushes up to the counter like he means to save me. "I'm fine," I say, when I really want to say, eff-off. But once again, I'm the idiot who wrote his name down.

"The first two numbers went to voicemail, so I just kept going down your list," the other flight instructor, a blond man wearing a White Sox hat, says, tapping my application. "Okay, next lessons will start soon, so let's get him checked out and prepare for the evening's work everyone."

I follow the health guy over to a corner and he listens to my heart rate and checks my pulse and blood pressure. "Kid, you got lucky," is what he leaves me with and then adds, "You're free to go. But you need to exit the premises with one of your emergency contacts. Is that clear?"

"Crystal," I say.

"So that's not your Dad?" Summer says, walking a half step behind me.

I don't answer.

"Wait up."

I don't.

"Fine. Happy to see you too."

Words that make me turn around. But she's already walking away in the opposite direction now.

I recognize her car in the parking lot. The same car she drove the night we met. Then she gets in her car, slams the door, and drives off. No goodbye. No wave. And no kiss blown in my direction.

A moment later, my phone buzzes from an incoming text, like a kick in the side when I feel like I'm already on the floor.

The message reads: If you wanted to leave me out of your life, next time, leave me off any list that matters.

As I watch her car disappear out of the parking lot, I think about her choice of one key word. Leave. The leaves tattoo on her arm. She means to leave the world changed. I just want everyone to leave me alone. I think. Because right now, I just wish she'd drive back, so I can rewind the clock and tell her a few things like:

Thanks for caring enough to come and check on me.
Or

You look so pretty in blue. You look amazing, even when you're mad.

Or

The reason I put you down on that list is because I have no one else. You're the one person apart from my sister who really matters.

I know that now.

~40~
Jesse

"You need a lift?" Uncle Billy approaches, shaking his car keys in his hands. "You can drive if you like? Sometimes it helps when you do something well after you mess up. At least that's been my experience."

I'm looking at him like he didn't just speak in English. I can't get a plane to leave the ground. I just passed out. And now he wants to give me the driver's seat. "You obviously do not value your life," I say and add, "No thanks."

"What? You don't have your license? But I thought in America, you only had to be sixteen?" Uncle Billy still follows me.

"Why don't you ask your big brother why I don't have my driver's license? Or why I've never flown a kite. Had a dog. Or gone to a Bulls game." I turn, not bothering to see his reaction. "Then get back to me."

"Look, Jesse," he says, "I'll just drive you out of the parking lot. So you don't forfeit your chances of coming back for future lessons. And even if you don't have your license, I'll coach you to back out and drive over to the exit." Uncle Billy points to a white pickup off by itself.

181

"Look, this is a huge lot. You won't hit another car unless you actually try to." When I stop walking and turn to face him, he asks, "You won't try to, will you? It's a rental."

He's right. They're probably watching me from the windows, and I need to leave accompanied. I agree to come. My plane never took off, but maybe I can make up for it with a little Nascar action. I settle for just driving slowly out of the lot so the flight school doesn't write me up for reckless driving too.

The car alarm beeps and the locks pop open on the Chevy S-10. "So the truck's a stick," Uncle Billy says. Maybe he meant, a cinch, as in easy to drive.

I get into the driver's seat, and he hands me the keys after he puts his seatbelt on. "All the American films I saw in Cape Town growing up had rowdy rich cowboys riding off into the sunset. And as far as I could tell, no one ever went for their driver's test in those films. Made me think boys in America were born knowing how to drive."

"Were they riding horses or sports cars?" I don't wait for his answer, but add, "I've played video games." A few of the free ones until Dad decided to cut off our access to the Internet back in high school.

"Sure. It's not too different." Uncle Billy points to the handle in the middle. "This here is your gearshift. The key to driving stick is to trust the feel of the engine more than watching the gauges. If the engine seems to be struggling, you need to downshift or shift up, depending on if you're slowing down or speeding up."

Sure. Got it. Not really, but how hard can it be, right? I rev the engine by pushing on the accelerator when Uncle Billy's hand goes up.

"You need to press the clutch before you shift gears, and when you start, it's good to have your foot on the brakes. Ease up, and then accelerate."

Clutch? I look down at my feet. Three pedals? "How do I remember which one's which?"

"The most important one is the middle one. The brakes." Uncle Billy puts his hand on the rod behind the gearshift. "This here is the parking brake, but while driving, you're in control of starting and stopping. If you stall out, which you probably will, more than three times, we'll switch seats. Because you'll strain the engine, and as I said before, this is a rental. If it were my car back home, you could drive it into a tree. No matter."

Three strikes. I get it. But I barely step off the brakes, shift into first gear, press the gas hard and stall out. Hitting the top of the steering wheel with a closed fist, I see Uncle Billy pull the parking brake up.

"Try easing off the clutch slowly, and you'll feel the moment when the car tells you to let go. Like dancing with a girl." Uncle Billy smiles, but I'm not discussing Summer.

"Like dancing with a girl," Uncle Billy repeats, "Sometimes you have to hold her close, and sometimes you have to let her go, do her twirl and then bring her back into your arms again. But you never totally let go, that way she always knows you're near."

The words sting, because I let Summer go. Why bother with strikes two and three? I feel like I've already struck out.

"Cheer up, chap." Uncle Billy says, tapping on the dash, "She'll come around."

And for a second, I can't tell if he's referring to the car or Summer. I take a deep breath and try again, this time trying to remember the part about easing up slowly. But no luck. I stall out again.

"Let me shift gears for you, and you just concentrate on the pedals." Uncle Billy's hand gently pushes mine off the gear, and then he lowers his window, looks back at the building, and waves the universal sign of don't worry. Everything's fine.

Every bone inside of me wants to say, "I don't need your help," but it's clear that I'm not a natural. Exhaling the voices of doubt in my head, I focus on the clutch and the accelerator, and after Uncle Billy releases the parking brake, I crank the engine to start again. Uncle Billy watches my feet closely, shifts, and says, "Okay, hit the clutch again," and when I press down, he shifts to gear two, and then he yells, "Hit the gas," and I do, and then I'm flying.

I'm really flying! I mean, driving. But it's such a rush as the truck pumps forward through the parking lot and my hands grip the steering wheel. I'm in control. I did it!

"You did it!" Uncle Billy says.

Nodding, I say, "Thanks, Daa—!" And then I catch myself, panic, and slam on the brakes, inches from the exit gate. And the truck stalls out again.

"It's okay," Uncle Billy says, "That was great for your first attempt! I'm proud of you. I really am!"

"I'm good," I say, putting the truck into park and exiting the Chevy. "Thanks," I say and walk off.

And he doesn't follow me. But before I get to the bus stop, my phone buzzes with a text from Uncle Billy. "Just so you know, any time you want another lesson, I'm happy to try again. Really. Any time."

I hold down on the edit option and delete the message.

The bus pulls up and as I step up onto it and take my seat, the phone buzzes with a call. It's Lagan's phone number. Tempted to ignore it but recalling that the flight school probably called them first, I pick it up.

"Jesse, are you okay?" It's Talia.

"Fine. Never been better?" Thankful she can't see

through the phone, I punch the seat once. Then again.

"Did everything work out? Did you fly?"

Thinking back to the rush I felt when the truck took off and I was driving, I smile to myself and decide the day wasn't a complete disaster and say, "Yep. Took off like lightning. Just have to work on landing."

"Don't we all," Talia says, and then she adds. "Want to invite Summer over for dinner? Rani brought over some spices, and she's gonna try to teach me how to make chicken tikka masala."

Summer. So wish I could. "I think I'll pass."

"On asking Summer or on coming to dinner? Or both?" Talia asks. "Because we should celebrate your first day flying."

"The plane never took off." I say, aware that I should have told her the truth in the first place.

"But you said—."

"I gotta go. I'll see you later. Going to look for a job. Don't wait up." And then I hang up. Because I have nothing to celebrate right now. Descending the bus and retracing my steps to the Blue line, and the brisk wind hits me like a slap in the face. It's not even the end of June and it feels like fall came early. And summer's gone.

41
~Talia~

Rani arrives with spices and several grocery bags, and Reggie swoops them off her hands the moment he sees her.

"So the deal is you guys disappear," Rani motions to Lagan and Reggie. "And when I text you, that'll be when dinner is served. Don't come back before that."

"Not even if the fire alarm sounds?" Lagan says, zipping up his backpack in the lounge, and when I punch him in the arm to save Rani the trouble, he laughs and says, "What?"

Reggie pulls Lagan toward the stairwell exit. Down the hallway, I overhear Reg say, "Why you gotta mess with my night off from cooking? Leggo."

When the guys are gone, I help Rani empty the food onto the kitchen counter and wait.

"So my mom always told me to tie my hair back when I'm on kitchen duty." She hands me her wrist that has a few hair ties wrapped around it.

I take a blue one and pull my hair back into a bun, say, "Thanks," and then wash my hands.

Spotting the onions, I start peeling and Rani says,

"Great. I'll marinate while you chop," and she dumps several chicken breasts into a steel bowl under the sink and rinses off the meat.

Working silently, I feel suddenly aware that this is the first time Rani and I have been alone, well, apart from the brief time the night of the police station incident. The closest thing I ever had to having a female friend was back in Kindergarten, but Dad put an end to that presto. My eyes sting, and I start sniffing.

Rani moves the chicken to the counter, washes her hands, and takes the plate of peeled onions and dumps them into a separate bowl, and puts it under the kitchen sink. Turning the water on, she says, "Mom taught me this trick about onions," while covering the onions with water.

"So you and your mom are close?" I ask, feeling unsure of what else to ask.

Rani doesn't answer right away as I watch her spoon several heaping spoons of plain yogurt over the chicken. While Rani stabs at the chicken repeatedly with a knife, she answers. "My mom and I are kind of not talking right now."

"Oh." And I feel stupid for asking. But I'm also confused.

"You're not gonna ask?" Rani says, peeling some fresh ginger and garlic now.

"It's none of my business." I'm chopping the onions now and my eyes don't hurt.

"Look." Rani stops peeling. "We might not ever be best friends, but I trust you. Because Lagan trusts you. So you can ask me anything."

I appreciate the trust, but I tell her honestly, "I don't know if I can say the same thing to you. I mean, I'm just not as open."

"That was pretty open of you to share," Rani says,

smiling while cutting up the ginger and garlic into fine pieces. "And for the record, Lagan has never told me anything about you, besides the constant reminder that he's sooooo in love with you."

Heat rises to my cheeks. I'm also reminded that Lagan did tell me a story about Rani. I take a deep breath and ask, "So why are you and your mom not speaking?"

"Long story," Rani says and we look at each other and crack up.

Opening up the spice tins, Rani looks at me and says, "I'm really bad with measuring out stuff. I just kind of put in a bit of this and a bit of that," and then she heaps spoons of turmeric, coriander, black pepper, cumin seeds and paprika over the yogurt-coated chicken.

After topping the mixture with minced garlic and ginger, she says. "Now this is the fun part," and pushes the bowl over in my direction. "Want to do the honors?"

I look down at my hands, and then holding the bowl steady with my left, I let my right dive into the cool yogurt and work the marinade into the chicken. Without thinking, the word, "Slimy," comes out of my mouth, and we're laughing again.

While I work at the chicken a bit more, Rani pours rice and water into a pot and turns on the burner at the back before pushing the pot over it.

"Another secret my mom taught me was to clean up as you go along." Rani rinses off the used bowls and knives and files them into the dishwasher.

If she's still talking about her mom, they'll probably figure it out.

After frying up the onions, ginger and garlic, Rani drops in the marinated chicken, mixes it up, and covers the pot. "Wow. That's wasn't so bad."

I look around and we've used up almost all the ingredients. "Thanks for doing this." I'm thinking of Lagan's smile when he takes his first bite.

"I wish relationships were like cooking. Just mix it all up, set it, and forget it," Rani says as I rinse off the dishes in the sink. "You realize your sleeves are getting wet, right?"

I don't answer. Right away. With my eyes on the running tap, I turn the cold water off and the steam of the hot water begins to rise up toward my face, and I move my hands out of the rising temperatures. "My dad used to take his anger out on me. On my arm." Turning the tap off, I file the dishes into the dishwasher as Rani turns the burners down to simmer, and we both get lost in our own thoughts while I wipe down the counter and Rani stirs the rice and then the chicken.

"I'm sorry about your Dad," Rani says. "Were things better with your mom? Did she believe you when you told her?"

"She died when I was twelve." Until I saw for myself, I never knew just how badly Dad was treating her.

Rani puts the ladle down on a clean dish and leans against the closed fridge. "I am so sorry. That just royally sucks."

Moments pass as I chop up the tomatoes.

Then Rani speaks. "I thought my mom and I were close. That I could tell her anything, and she'd believe me. Apparently I was wrong." Rani's eyes meet mine before she adds, "I mean, why would anyone lie about something so wrong, right?"

I don't know. But I kinda know. At least I think I know.

When she says, "Lagan told me that he told you," I realize I do know.

I know exactly what she's referring to. "I'm sorry," I say, averting my gaze back to the pots on the stovetop. My appetite leaves me as I think about how Rani's mom didn't believe that her uncle molested her.

"Maybe I should have said something sooner." Rani's voice trails off.

There are no words to say in moments like this. How do you fight a battle when only one person sees the enemy? It's so lonely, and I can only imagine how broken Rani must feel, like someone's trying to erase her story.

"It's not like I can prove it." And then she glances at my wet sleeves and says, "I am so sorry. That was uncalled-for."

"It's okay." I don't need to punish her for what happened to me. Just reminds me that we all have scars. But not all of us have scars that others can see. "Do you think sometimes it's just not worth it?"

Without hesitation, she says, "I'm still glad I told her, because I'm free from the secret I've been carrying around all these years. It's not my fault that my mom doesn't believe me. We can only control so much, ya know?"

I do know.

Turning the rice off, Rani asks me to bring over the chopped tomatoes. When the chicken breaks off with the side of a fork, I top the curry with tomatoes as Rani pours in a cup of heavy cream.

"Voila." Rani says, and turns the burner down to simmer. "Ten more minutes and we should text the boys to come back for the meal of their lives!"

"Thanks for sharing with me," I say, not wanting to miss the moment.

Rani looks up from her phone. "I know you have Lagan and Jesse, but if you, I dunno, ever need some girl time…"

"Thanks."

We set the table in the lounge and Lagan and Reggie show up with soda, sparkling cider and smiles.

Rubbing his belly, Reggie says, "I hope you made enough for seconds. I can tell already that I will be having some."

"After me, dude," Lagan playfully pushes Reggie behind him, and Reggie says, "After you," and the two of them take over serving food onto each of our plates.

"Dig in," Rani says, giving the guys permission to start, and we watch each other take a spoonful of steaming chicken and rice.

We're eating silently, chewing slowly, and I gulp down a huge sip of cider to cool my tongue. I'm probably the one here who can't handle a little spice. Then Reggie gulps down his whole cup. Followed by Lagan who doesn't put his cup down till it's empty. Rani spits her mouthful into her napkin, turns to face us, and says, "What's the number for that pizza place that delivers?" and we all start laughing.

Thinking back to what Lagan's mom had said to me, Rani and I both conclude that she mixed up the paprika with the chili pepper.

But I don't sleep well that night, replaying Rani's story and worrying even more that there's not enough evidence to prove Dad really hurt Jesse and me. What if the jury, like Rani's mom, doesn't believe me? And all night long, the mother who hardly spoke to me when she was around follows me in my dreams, repeating two words: "Why bother?"

42
~Jesse~

Back on the train, I lean back and resort to searching for job opportunities from the posters, but they're all happy faces, advertising colleges and dreaming big. I resort to closing my eyes and thinking about my next meal. Making a note to avoid bananas this time, I decide to google if churros have potassium. For no reason, I tell myself. Just to know, I tell myself. But I can't get her outta my mind.

Even the leaves blowing on the trees outside the train window seem to be whispering subliminal messages too. "Idiot, why'd you ever leave her to begin with?"

As I exit the train and make my way down to the street, I think about how I can't even plan my next flying lesson till I go back to Dr. Singh and get medical clearance. I wonder if Summer learned about acute renal failure in her textbooks yet. If she had been with me, she probably would have reminded me not to eat that stupid banana.

Walking up to the library, I look around me, startled by how I got here. Like I was on autopilot, but I know I can't go in there. She obviously doesn't want to see me nor have anything to do with me. The Churro Guy's within earshot, but I'm not going over there. I can't be that guy who leaves messages with churro vendors till I grow old and grey.

Planting myself on a park bench at Millennium Park, I stare at the phone, and maybe because you can't see faces when you type into a phone, I pull up the contacts and type, "About that example of dancing with a girl?" And hit send. Then I wait, because I need this advice soon, and if Uncle Billy's too busy for me, whatever. I'll figure it out on my own, but ellipses show up, and by now, I know that means he's typing back.

"Ask away. I took lessons back in Cape Town. I'm pretty good, actually." The text comes back. I could never imagine Dad dancing with Mom. Or dancing. Period.

I take a deep breath and type, You said some stuff about letting go but staying nearby. What about when you step on her toes? And hurt her feelings.

You could start by saying, you're sorry—the reply comes back. And then give it a little time, and ask her to dance again.

But what if it's not the first time you stepped on her toes? I message.

When he asks, Is her toe bruised or broken? I feel exposed. He's asking without asking how badly I've hurt her, and I don't know for sure, but from the way she drove off, I'm thinking broken. Definitely broken.

I'm just a bad dancer, I message back, because I'm afraid to type a word that starts with B. Summer had her B words she shared with her siblings. Until this moment, I never put together that B words mark the story or my

193

life. Mine. Talia's. Mom's. Words like:

Burnt. Bruised. Bleeding. Broken. Bad.

That's when I realize it's too late. I wrote, bad. I guess I'm not as good at hiding as I think I am. And Uncle Billy doesn't respond right away either. And the ellipses disappear and I sigh. He's giving up on me too, and he should. Didn't take much for him to figure out I'm a loser, but just when I'm about to put the phone away, words come up on the screen. A whole paragraph actually.

Dancing is the easy part. But dancing with someone is hard. And hard work. Trust me on this one, girls expect us guys to screw up. But what they hope for more, is that we'll keep trying. And that we won't give up trying. And fighting for them. That's how they know they matter to us. I asked, bruised or broken, because the latter will take more time to heal, but that's okay. Some hurts take longer than others in life to heal, and sometimes we still have scars. And they could remind us of how much we've been hurt in the past. Or scars can remind us that we're on our way to healing. And how far we've come. Make sense?

I swat the corner of my eye. And tug my shirt down at the back, glancing left and right to make sure no one saw the rogue tear that tried to escape. And without knowing, I'm re-reading Uncle Billy's words and nodding. Because it does make sense. I just hope he's right.

I type the word, Thanks, and then without thinking, I type my old address down, the one where we last lived in Darien. Then add, That's the place Dad tried his best to break me. And flippantly add, In case you're wondering.

Because just when I thought I was talking about Summer, somehow the dance became the one between a

194

parent and a child. Between a father and a son. Between me and the dad I wish I had. And I push past several people crowding now to take pictures under the Millennium Park coffee bean, because I feel a flood rising in my throat.

And Mom, I know you're not here, but I still can't swim and I feel like I might drown. Right here, right now. I'm drowning. And the last thing I need is a mirror to show me what I can't hide. I'm alone. And I know that I don't want to be.

43
~Jesse~

Seven days crawl by as I wallow in my failures. Mope
around. Avoid Talia and the rest of them. Job hunt
unsuccessful. No affordable place yet either. And I leave
the phone off and in my pocket. Eat very little. Walk
past the Churro Guy, but I never buy a churro.

Pulling off a leaf from a tree, I press it carefully in
between a library book I checked out before Summer
and I had our falling out. I use the leaf as a bookmark,
but I read the same passages over and over again, unable
to concentrate. I debate asking Uncle Billy if he'll take
me out driving, just so I can think about something
besides Summer and the last words she said to me. But I
don't want to encourage him. It still eats at me that he'd
want to help Dad in any way.

Day after day, I drift near but never actually up the
library door. And then a week goes by and I have to
return the book. It's overdue tomorrow, so an hour
before the library's due to close, I reason that I have no
choice. I have to go in. But before I do, I gain the

courage to text Summer two words:

I'm sorry.

But she doesn't respond. Maybe she doesn't have her phone with her, I tell myself, when I push through the front doors of the library. Maybe she can't get good reception in the library. Or her phone battery ran out and she forgot to bring her charger, I assure myself, when I push the book through the slot marked for returned books.

Or maybe she's done. Over me. And she's moved on. Just one peek to see if she's studying in her usual cubicle, and I promise to let it go. As much as it hurts, I have to let her go.

I recognize her sweater hanging on the back of the chair, but she's nowhere in sight. A physics textbook lies open, and from a quick glance, she's studying formulas that may as well be French to me. Sheesh. What a brainiac.

Glancing around and not seeing her, I quickly pick up her pen, turn her notebook to a clean page, and scrawl the two words I texted her earlier. Then click her pen shut and flip the page back to the one I thought she was on. Instead I find a different page. A page with my name on it, and a list of words numbered one to ten. Dated, "The day Jesse brought me flowers."

1. Kind
2. Cute
3. Funny
4. Thoughtful
5. Generous
6. Patient
7. Quiet, but in the best way
8. Did I mention cute already?
9. Dreamer - Just doesn't know it yet

10.   Future pilot. Can't wait to watch him fly!

The words stun me like a game of freeze tag. The game Talia used to egg me on to play when we were done with our chores. Then one day, my legs stopped moving.

I can't believe she wrote this about me. I can't believe she thinks this about me. Correction: thought.

She's now walking toward me, her hands rubbing her arms like she's shivering. I feel frozen in time. She's wearing black from head to toe. And I feel somehow responsible.

"I thought you were outside," she says. "I shoulda brought my jacket with me."

You went looking for me? Glad she didn't bring her sweater, because that's how I knew she was here. I look in those blue eyes, and they're soft and inviting, and remind me that she's not wearing all black today after all.

"Say something." She leans in and then when I don't, she brushes by and scoots into her seat. "I guess I should just go back to studying." Then she flips a page of her textbook and picks up her pen. I can't see her eyes any more, like the curtains closed and night is here. I make to leave, unsure of how to talk to her. Unsure of how to make this work. And if this is a dance, I am completely lost as to what the next step should be.

Then I notice Summer's hand covering the words I wrote on her notebook. She looks up and holds her phone toward me, her eyes like cloudy blue skies now. "One more time, and I think I might actually believe you."

A bald guy wearing glasses looks up from his newspaper and gives us the evil eye. I motion to

Summer to come outside with me. I'll say it one more time, but I don't want to be kicked out of the library in the process. As she rises from her chair, I pull her sweater off the back and drape it over her shoulders. I saw it in a movie once. Then when we get to the door, I open it and stand back, like Uncle Billy did for her when we left the flight school.

Once we're outdoors, I remember that I forgot the leaf I had saved for her in the book I dropped off. "Wait here a second," I say and race back to the return bin.

"Any chance I could just get something from a book I put in there a little while ago? I forgot, umm, a bookmark in it."

The African-American librarian pulls her chair up to the counter and turns to face her computer screen. "Name, please."

"Introduction to Flight," I say, turning to see if Summer followed me back inside. She didn't. But I can also see what I think is the corner of the book through the slot. It's on the top of the pile.

"No. Your name?" the woman asks.

"Jesse…I mean John… I mean Lagan—"and I reach into the slot, but she clears her throat and shakes her head no. Not allowed.

"I'll page one of the volunteers to come and look through this bin and see if it's still in here or in transition."

She picks up her phone.

"It's. Right. There." And what exactly does 'in transition' mean?

"Someone will be free in half an hour. Come back then."

Seriously? I could scratch up my hand and just reach in there and pull the book out, but from the look of Madam Librarian, she'll call security. Hands shoved in my jacket pocket, I walk back outdoors and Summer's spinning on her heels left and right, tugging her sweater over her hands.

"Sorry to keep you waiting."

Summer throws her arms around my neck. "That counts. Let's go back inside. I'm freeeezing!"

I could keep you warm. Pulling her closer, I look into her eyes, round like twin turquoise pools, and say the words I've been practicing all week in my head. "I'm sorry for letting you go. I thought I could leave you. Fix my life, and then find you again."

She's looking in my eyes and blinks, steps back and asks, "Why'd you go back in there anyway?"

"A leaf," I say, shrugging my shoulders. "There was this leaf I had kinda, sorta, saved for you all week."

"A leaf, huh?" She asks and she looks upward. We're not standing under a tree, but a few stars dot the Chicago sky. "What made this particular leaf so special? Was it purple?" Summer asks.

Laughing, I make a note to find a purple leaf some day when I fly to the various corners of the world. If one exists, I'll save it for her. "It made me think of you."

Summer smiles, inching closer again, and time stops. Or so it seems. And I have to ask her. I need to know. "The list? The one you made about me. Is it true? Do you still think that about me?"

She answers by moving closer still. And then she kisses me. Or I kiss her. I can't quite tell who kissed who on the lips first. But if this is dancing, I'm in favor of practicing that last move. Often.

44
~Talia~

All week Jesse is nowhere to be found. He leaves before I wake up. He doesn't return until after I've gone to sleep. But I'm learning to let go. And not baby my brother who's becoming a man. He's got some stuff to sort out. That's the obvious part. And I have to trust that he'll talk to me when he needs to.

All of us want to keep distracted from the impending trial, so we each do what we do best. The campus library posts a job opening which a friend of Reggie's helps me snag. Grateful for an upcoming paycheck, I also sign out books I have to read for my fall classes. Every little bit saved helps.

Lagan plays basketball in between trying to crash my journaling sessions and doing his own studying. Reggie plugs away at pre-med classes, showing off his knowledge every chance he gets, like his witty rundown on skin cells the time I got a pesky paper cut. And Rani hangs around, and we chat books when one of us goes on a study break. She also teaches me a few more recipes, after we clearly mark the paprika and chili powder tins. I can tell from how often she sits near

Reggie that something might be starting between the two of them. We can all tell.

The days fly by but the nights linger—my insomnia has worsened ever since Rani told me about her mom. Tossing and turning, the phone next to my pillow teases me each time I wake up. I finally resolve to place a call.

Luke answers on the first ring, his voice a little groggy.

"Did I wake you up?" I ask, afraid I misjudged how long I slept. Or rather how long I've been awake.

"It's only 4:30 in the morning. What's up?"

Oops. "Sorry, let me call you back in a few hours."

"Talia," Luke says, "I'm awake now. What did you want?"

"I had a question about evidence." I pause. "Do we have enough?"

"I think I know where you're going with this." Luke's voice perks up. "You want to search your house again? If so, I can put in for a repeat search warrant, but it's rare that investigators will find anything new."

"Sorry for the timing of my call," I say, "And thanks. Thanks for everything."

"No worries. You know I could charge you double for this call? But..." Luke laughs softly. "I won't. Because I like you and your brother. I'll talk to you soon, okay. Bye for now."

"Bye," I say, and turn over to catch a few more z's, but I can't shut my mind off, so I climb down from the loft and find a pair of leggings and my runners in the dark, settling for a pair of Jesse's socks from our mishmash of stuff. If we were outdoors, lugging these garbage bags around would make us look like we were homeless. The word homeless stings somewhere deep inside me, and I wonder if I'll even really know what home looks like. Feels like. Smells like.

Jody, the woman in charge of the second shelter, taught me the value of an early morning jog, and I can only hope that a little fresh air will help with stress management. After finding a Post-it on Lagan's desk to leave him and Jesse a note, I pocket the phone, crank the door open slowly, and close it behind me. I plan to be back before anyone wakes up, but just in case I get sidetracked, I don't want them to worry. Finding Lagan's ear buds in his sweatshirt pocket, I tiptoe down the hallway to the stairwell and out into the pre-dawn morning.

Thankful for music to keep me company, I find Lagan's library of songs and scroll over the heading marked Playlists. "Dewdrops" it is.

Adjusting the ear buds, I pull the hood over my head, turn the volume up but press pause and take a moment to stretch. Moving across the street to keep from being swept up by a roaring street cleaner, I press play and a giggle escapes as the first song comes to life in my ears: the prom theme song we danced to in the mall between the racks of Forever 21. And as I start a slow trot toward Lake Michigan, I let my mind wander to that day back in Senior year. The shades Lagan placed on me before we left the parking lot. The three dresses he made me try on. The shimmery crown he placed in my hair. My head on his shoulder. His lips pressed on my skin.

When Savage Garden's song fades, a song I don't recognize plays, but the words remind me of a certain string of white lights Lagan sent me in the shelter. The ones he asked to hang on the wall in a Z-shape to mimic lightning, and went on in a letter to describe my "lightning eyes." If we started with clouds, and moved to lightning, a date away from the city might replace those storms with stars.

The third song to play begins with a pretty piano intro and mentions stars in the first line. I quickly glance down. It's a song by a band named, Coldplay. Okay. I like it.

And maybe I imagine it, but I swear when I look up, a falling star races across the sky in an instant, making me come to a panting stop and stare where I believe I saw it. No one will ever believe me.

It was just for you, the gardener whispers to me, and if he means to remind me that someone out there thinks about me while the rest of the world sleeps, I'll take it.

45
~Talia~

When I hit the Lake, I turn the music off, tuck the ear buds away, and pause to catch my breath. Finding a park bench, I sit by the water and watch the sunrise. The red line on the water meets me just like the first time with Jody. It's just me and the sun, and I'm reminded of the bridge Luke mentioned, hoping that we'll make it over the waves.

Rising to my feet, I take a long hard look at the sun-line and then push myself against the morning wind, following the curve of Lake Shore Drive, no sailboats on the water yet. Running past Navy Pier, the seats on the Giant Ferris Wheel swing with the breeze coming off the water, and I tighten the strings of my hoodie to minimize the cold air sneaking in to make icicles of my ears.

Dawn pushes back the night as a bird flutters across the lake, plunging her head in, and flying off with her breakfast of some small fish. Reminding me that I started running on empty, and if I don't start heading back, I'll cramp up. Glancing ahead, several police cars with their flashing lights blazing line up next to each other, cutting off traffic on part of Lake Shore Drive, sealing the deal for me to turn around.

As I face North Chicago and pick up my pace, I think of all the women I met in the shelter. One by one, I picture their faces, the sound of their voices, the music of their laughter. And then, I whisper their names into the wind and recall their stories.

And then I think of Diana and Jody, two women dedicated to love and nurture us back to write new chapters of our stories. Diana who reminded me that someday, it would be my turn to tell my story. Jody, who helped me to file the restraining order against Dad. How different my life would be if I hadn't left the house and met each of these ladies?

As I jog up the final two blocks, I start cramping, so I slow down to walk the final stretch, massaging the sides of my waist, but when my eyes catch the headlines of the morning paper behind a glass-cased stand, I crumble to my knees on the sidewalk. The bold print reads, "MOD Witness Killed in Cab Accident" above a picture of a car ablaze on Lake Shore Drive.

Without any quarters, I can't retrieve a copy, but I read as much as I can through the window.

"Fiery flames filled the sky as a tragic car accident gridlocked traffic on Lake Shore Drive. EMTs and firefighters rushed to the scene, working to contain the fire and rescue the parties involved. Ambulances rushed a 42-year old male cabbie and a young woman to Northwestern Hospital late last night after the cab flipped and crashed into the Lake Shore Drive median. Both passengers were pronounced dead on arrival.

The cab driver's 17-year-old daughter told reporters, "My dad was working a bunch of extra shifts to pay for my prom and dress and he was worried about college tuition coming up next year." With tear-filled eyes, the daughter said, "Who cares about prom! I just want my dad back."

The other victim was a woman not much older than the cabbie's daughter. For weeks, her identity remained private during the ongoing investigation of MOD hotels, and what was predicted to become one of Chicago's biggest trials of this decade. Now the primary witness in the trial and the CEO whom she stabbed are both deceased. The CEO recently died from complications in the hospital after surgery. A press conference will be held this afternoon to announce the possible calling off of the investigation and the undetermined postponement of any pending trials related to the case.

"Attorney Gerard Vanderbilt, representing MOD hotels, was unavailable for comment. The renowned lawyer facing his own…"

That's all I'm able to read, the rest of the story must be on a different page, and my bottom lip stings from me biting down so hard on it. Forcing myself to rise from the pavement, I shove the back of my hand to my mouth to keep myself from breaking skin, but it's too late. I taste the trickle of blood from my lip as I find my way back to Lagan's dorm with one name piercing my thoughts. One face, whose story I'll never forget. One woman, who shared the love of blue with me. *Jaya.*

46
~Talia~

When I stumble into the lounge and plop onto the
single empty sofa chair, Reggie's eyes are glued to the
TV, a morning talk show host interviewing some guy in
scrubs about some medical breakthrough. Coffee is
apparently good for you, again.

"Hey, you went for a run?" Reggie says, but his
attention is still on the screen, the hosts clinking coffee
mugs with the medical expert.

I don't answer, but as Lagan and Jesse stir from
sleep, I realize my brother slept on a couch rather than
Reggie's bed. The TV host shifts the conversation. "And
now for the local news and a look at your morning
commute. How are the roads on this beautiful Chicago
day, Judy?"

Lake Shore Drive lies behind the female reporter
who says, "Well, Barbara, the crews are just finishing up
with clearing the damage from last night's car fire, and I
just got word that LSD should be up and clear before
the 7:00AM rush. We've got blue skies and 75 degrees.
Should be a beautiful day."

The camera shifts to a news anchor back in the

studio, a blazing fire projected behind him on a screen. "And that deadly car crash last night killed a 42-year-old cabbie and a dedicated father, and the primary witness of the upcoming MOD Hotels trial. What do you think the infamous Gerard Vanderbilt will think of the news, Judy?"

"Well, Jim, we tried to call and talk to him, but Attorney Vanderbilt, for once, has, quote, 'no comment.'"

I rise to shut the TV off. Dad's probably too busy gloating to speak right now. The one person who planned to speak up against the trafficking charges is gone.

"Wasn't that your dad they were—" Reggie stops mid-sentence. Jesse punches the couch. And Lagan moves over to sit on the armrest of my chair.

I can't see my eyes, but they should be black, in mourning. For Jaya.

"For once, I wish someone else would get a frickin' break. Just once." Jesse curses as he throws his hands behind his head and leans back on the couch.

"Did you know her?" Lagan asks.

I nod, but I wonder to myself, does anyone really know anyone that well? I knew chaos, pain and disappointment accompanied her every step. But this trial might have been her second chance. A springboard to start over.

"Maybe what we need to be asking is could someone have really orchestrated that kind of accident? To get rid of a witness." Drawing quotation marks in the air with his fingers when he said, "get rid of," Reggie adds, "That would be seriously cray!"

"How would you go about proving something like that?" Lagan says.

"If it was a hit and run, another car would have

yellow paint marks on it somewhere, to show the impact of the cab." Jesse punches his hands together and says, "BAM! Flip! Wham!"

A woman died. More like a girl. I don't know that any of this even matters. Rising to go back in Lagan's room, I decide maybe a shower will help me think through things. A place I can be alone. The warm water, my trusted friend that weeps with me, and no one stops me as I leave the lounge and push myself through the motions.

Where are your pictures now, Jaya? What color were you thinking during your last breath? Red for blood? Orange for the flames? Or just black? For the darkness you saw when you closed your eyes for the very last time.

Dressed, I look out Lagan's window, one or two early bird students hustling back and forth, backpacks in tow. I could make my way to the library and start reading ahead and offer to work an extra shift. I could cook up some eggs for everyone, giving Chef Reggie a break. Or I could find a Laundromat and help keep Jesse's and my dirty clothes from piling up.

"Dewdrop for your—."

"Not now." Seeing his eyes lowered, I feel bad for cutting Lagan off. Towel drying my hair, I resolve to express a few of my thoughts. "I wonder who will go to her funeral. I wonder who will plan it. I wonder if my Dad will be there, just to put on a good show."

"I'm so sorry, Talia." Lagan hugs me from behind, his arms crossing over in front of me, his hands holding my arms. "I'll go with you, if that's what you're asking."

"You know, no one came to my mom's funeral. Not one person outside of Jesse, Dad and me. And the guys who worked at the cemetery, but that doesn't count."

"I'm glad I went with you to visit her gravesite." Lagan pauses. "Thanks for sharing that part of you with me."

"But... it's so far away. I have nothing, not one thing, to remind me of her."

Lagan runs a hand over my head and down my hair. "You have her hair."

"It's not the same. I mean, even my memory of what she looked like seems fuzzy these days, like I can't see her face clearly. Was it round? Was it oval? Was she smiling?"

"There are a thousand pictures of me with my parents. I can't imagine how hard it is not to have even one." Lagan says, brushing a soft kiss on my forehead.

A knock at the door and Jesse's looking up at the ceiling. "Didn't mean to interrupt."

"You're cool," Lagan says, moving next to me so I can face Jesse.

"I saw Summer last night." Jesse's smiling, and I feel like I notice a pep in his step.

"And?" I ask, glad for the tiny distraction.

"And...I think she likes me."

Jesse's grin is the best thing I've seen in a long time.

"What's not to like?" I'm talking about Jesse, but typical Lagan. He's pointing to himself.

"And I've been thinking about Uncle Billy."

The glance Lagan and I exchange can only be summarized as whoa! Double whoa really. "You're calling him Uncle, now?"

"Anyway, I think it's time we told him some stuff. Are you up for a field trip?"

"Did you already ask him? Where and when?" I leave off the question why.

"It's not till this afternoon. At our house in Darien. He said yes."

"You want to go back there?" Lagan asks. "Are you sure it's safe? Besides, the charges were dropped, but not that long ago."

"If you're worried about our Dad, I'm guessing he doesn't come around much. He hates anything unclean, and after the job I did…"

"I thought I'd never wanna go back there, but…" I take a deep breath and continue. "No one lives there now. It would give me a chance to look for a picture of Mom."

"The only one Dad kept was the portrait by the front door. And T., I'm sorry. I'm sure I ruined it."

My heart sinks.

"I don't know." Lagan puts his hands on my shoulders. "Sometimes that kind of stuff can be salvaged if we ask a professional. Someone who works with restoring photographs."

No one can restore Jaya's life. "I have to call Diana. And find out if they're doing a service for Jaya." I face Lagan. "I'd like it if you came with me." And then I look my brother in the eyes. "And you too."

"Well, I'll be coming with you today, so get used to me, Dewdrop."

"The girl's dad arrested you once for trespassing," Reggie's standing in the doorway. "Sorry I overheard, but do you really think it's a good idea to go back there?"

"It'll just be Talia and me." Jesse's not asking for permission. He moves to take his toothbrush off the shelf. "It's a family thing we have to do. That's all. And we lived there, so it wouldn't be trespassing, correct?"

"I guess…" Reggie says, his uncertainty mirroring Lagan's hesitation as he hands Jesse the key I gave him months ago.

"You don't plan to stay there long, right?" Lagan's asking.

"Just long enough to show Uncle Billy around." Jesse

looks right at me. Right at my arm.

"Fine," Lagan complies, adding, "But we're gonna camp out nearby in case something goes down. Keep your cell on you."

Jesse answers, "Fair enough."

47

~Talia~

The house looks pretty much the same from the outside, although the police roped off the perimeter with caution tape.

"You think we should ask the neighbors if they've seen Dad come around?" I can feel my heart pounding as we draw closer, even with Jesse by my side. "I mean, it couldn't hurt to ask."

"Sure." Either Jesse can't tell, or he's kind enough not to draw attention to the fact that I'm delaying.

Jesse rings the doorbell of the neighbors on the right, waits, then rings again. No one comes to the door. Moving to the house on the other side, same thing happens, and the paranoid side of me worries some people are inside, but they don't want to talk to us.

"They probably recognize us and don't want anything to do with the strange kids who've been in the news," my brother says.

"People just don't like strangers. Period." I'm one of those people.

"I get it. They don't want any more Girl Scout Cookies." Jesse shrugs his shoulders and says, "Forget it.

Let's go."

After another moment, I turn to walk down the porch when I hear the sound of the front door opening. "Hello. Can I help you with something?" A tall, pregnant, blond I don't recognize carries a wailing infant in her arms.

"Umm," I can barely hear myself think over the crying. "We were just wondering if anyone lives next door anymore?"

She's bouncing the baby on her hip now, and the little one's volume simmers from a roar to a sniffling whimper. "Oh that place? We just moved in, and I haven't seen anyone come by there in quite some time. Someone told me the family was a bit strange, but not to worry, they aren't coming back. Why? Are you looking to buy it?"

"Actually, we used to live there," Jesse says from the bottom of the porch steps.

I glare at my brother. Did he not hear the woman use the word strange to describe us?

And then Jesse adds, "But we don't anymore."

The baby's wailing again, perhaps sensing the tension in the air. "Thanks for your time," I say, "My brother and I just wanted to see if a few of our things were still in the house." And then I turn to leave, not waiting for Jesse to set another fire for me to put out.

As we walk side by side down one walkway, across the yard, and back up the driveway to the house we lived in, I mumble under my breath. "Great. Now she'll probably call the cops on us."

"Not if she believes we live here. That would be silly." Jesse raises his eyebrows playfully as we carefully step between the caution tape which has taken a hit from the summer rains. "Plus, something tells me she'll be busy for at least an hour to get that kid to stop crying."

"Good point." I glance back, but mommy and baby are no longer in sight.

"And look on the bright side," he says, turning the key in the front door and pushing it open. "At least good ol' Dad didn't change the locks on us."

"That's the last thing I'll ever call him."

Jess dismisses me and says, "Uncle Billy should be here any minute."

My feet feel glued to the floorboards, my senses taking it all in. Jesse wasn't kidding when he said he did some number with the gasoline. My sense of smell gets slammed first.

"I feel like we walked into an abandoned gas station." I flip the light switch, but no light turns on. And things are missing. Like the couch. Curtains. The carpeting.

"Looks like the power's been cut." Jesse says. He's in the kitchen.

As Jesse moves on down the hall, I'm guessing he's headed to the office, but I still can't move. Because the walls are saturated with voices.

"Count to ten, Talia!" Dad's voice booms. "Start over Talia! Slower this time."

I clench my left arm to me and squeeze my eyes shut.

"Clean up the closet, Talia!" Dad says. "And your mother too. What a mess she made! And it better be all clean when I get back, or else!"

The door to the nearest closet is shut. I think I'll ask Jesse to search the closets for me.

"There's no time for stories," Mom says, "Your Dad will be home soon. Hurry. Get your homework done. Do your chores. We can't take a chance." And then she did. Two minutes with the neighbors. Sharing a fruit salad Jesse and I chopped up. And the rest is a part of history I wish I could forget.

"Talia!" Jesse calls from somewhere in the house. "Come here."

Exhaling, I force myself to move from the front door, no little papers numbered one to ten on the little table, now knocked over. When I find Jesse looking through Dad's filing cabinet, there's broken glass everywhere.

"Did you do this?"

"It was locked." Jesse walks over to give me a hand over the debris. I take it, bending to keep my hair from snagging on the jagged edges.

"All the papers in the files," Jesse says, "They're gone."

"Well, what'd you expect?" He brought me over here to tell me this.

"I dunno, but I wish I had taken some of them with me. Maybe they meant something."

"Dad doesn't save anything. You would know that except you didn't have to pack when we left Michigan." The words slip out and I feel like a jerk. "Sorry, I just meant…"

"I screwed up," Jesse says, moving to the stairwell. With one hand on the railing, he turns and says, "Not a day goes by when I wish I had been more there for you, T."

"You're here for me now." I step closer, and put my hand softly on his back. "That's all that matters."

Jesse walks over to the front door, picking up the little table that used to hold the lists, pats the elephants covering the wooden top. "But he did save furniture. I remember this from when I was like three."

I walk over to the living room and touch the top of the couch. "Yeah. And this couch. None of us hardly sat on this couch, and Dad saved it and dragged it with us to Chicago." Suddenly pictures of Mom going about her routine of chores, dusting a familiar chair, holding a kitchen towel, and making the bed flood my mind.

There's only one time Mom deviated from her routine and didn't get caught. When my third grade teacher got engaged. She let me tell her a long story. We giggled. It was a moment we shared exchanging secrets. Pinky promises and all.

"Wait!" I don't want to say more in case I'm wrong.

I carefully inch back out of Dad's office and race past Jesse's mangled wheelchair at the bottom of the staircase, up the steps to Dad's bedroom. Jesse follows. I stop inches from where Dad slept. The pillows are gone and from a quick glance so are the clothes in the closet.

Jesse's arm brushes mine when he catches up. "What?"

"Help me lift this, Jess." The mattress isn't that heavy but I need my hands free so I can look under it.

After pulling all the covers and sheets off, my brother raises the mattress, I feel around all the edges underneath and find nothing. Just when I resolve to give up, I think of Jaya and I can't. Not yet. "Let's flip it over. Just in case it got shifted during the move."

Jessie complies, knocking over a table lamp that makes a dull thud on the carpeted floor. As he puts it back on the nightstand, Jesse asks, "You still haven't told me what we're looking for?"

The plastic covering on the mattress is a discolored yellow, and there's no way to see through it, so I pat down the mattress, inch by inch and near the middle left, I feel something. Ripping a hole in the lining, I pull out the treasure Mom showed me when I was a little girl.

Holding a magazine, I hand it to Jesse. "This. This is what I was looking for."

Jesse flips through it and tosses it back in my arms. "What? Did Mom look at this to make herself feel better, because Dad never treated her like this?"

The journal looks greyed and many pages are bent and curled as I turn them, one by one, till I find it. She's wearing a sari, the color faded from the bright royal blue of my memories, like clouds rolled over her one sunny day. And never left. But she's the most beautiful woman on the page. In the whole book.

Jesse's looking over my shoulder now as I run my fingers over the caption. "It really is her? I see her face, but I'm not sure. Did we know her? Did we ever really have a mom?" Jesse's questions cut deep, but the label under Mom's name cuts deeper.

Escort.

And this time, I know exactly what that word means.

48
~Jesse~

Talia hugs the magazine as she leans against the dresser while I flip the mattress upright and replaces it on the box spring.

When I lift a corner of the bed, she looks at me and says, "I can't. I want to keep it. It's the only thing I have from Mom. I need it."

I wasn't sure. I mean, it's Mom's picture, but it's also a catalogue. I figured that much out by the caption and the prices everywhere. "Do you really want to remember her like this?" I drop the mattress.

"Do you think she had a choice?" Talia pauses. "They were poor. Her parents thought she'd have a better life." Then her voice trails off. We both know Mom found the exact opposite.

"Here, let me take a picture of it. And of the pages Mom's on. That way we'll always have it." I want to crop out the description and the dollar sign, and leave just Mom's face. Her beautiful smile. That's the part I want to keep.

Talia places the magazine on the edge of the bed and I pull out my phone, but hand it to my sister. There are a bunch of missed texts and calls from Lagan. Most of them asking if we're okay. She texts back, yes, and then finds the camera function. As Talia takes the pictures, I flip the pages to find Mom's face, and lay the magazine down flat again.

"Hello?" a voice calls from downstairs. "Sorry, I'm late."

I motion to Talia. "He's here." Picking up the magazine, the two of us make our way downstairs to meet Uncle Billy.

Billy's wearing his cowboy boots and jeans again, but this time he's wearing a cowboy hat too. Maybe he thinks all Americans dress like that.

"You're not that late." I shake hands with him.

Talia's expression of confusion reminds me. I told her I saw Summer, but I never mentioned Uncle Billy and the pseudo dance lessons. Or the kiss.

When Uncle Billy hands ice cream to Talia, "I thought we could grab some burgers later. If you like."

My sister's smile looks forced and she steps back like she means to keep her distance. We all stand there for a moment. The silence doesn't seem to bother Uncle Billy as he turns his head slowly, taking it all in.

"Should we start the tour in the kitchen?" I say, and Uncle Billy and Talia follow me. This was my idea, after all.

Placing the magazine on the counter, I pick the teakettle off the floor, put it on the stovetop, then turn to Uncle Billy. "Now close your eyes and imagine a young girl making tea." Uncle Billy glances from me to Talia—back to me. Then complies.

"Mugs line the countertop. The teakettle whistles. The chores haven't been done on time. And a young boy, the girl's brother, is stuck in a wheelchair. Before the girl can pour hot water into the cups, an angry dad shows up and—"

"Stop!" Talia screams, and Uncle Billy opens his

eyes.

"What is it?" Billy asks. "I know you're talking about Geri. What did he do?"

Talia stares at the teakettle, looks me in the eyes, then leaves the ice cream on the kitchen table, and walks over to the sink, stretching her arm over it.

And as I hold an empty, tilting teakettle over her arm, Talia pulls up her sleeve, and I hear Uncle Billy curse under his breath. He moves nearer, but she pulls her sleeve down before his outstretched hand touches her scars.

"The bastard told me you were clumsy," Uncle Billy says. "He told me you would try to trick the courts and make up stories about him. We've heard of a few cases of American kids suing their parents over stupid things. Geri told me you and your brother were doing that too."

"Clumsy? That's what he called my sister?" I throw the teakettle against the wall, storm out of the kitchen and head upstairs. I can hear footsteps racing to catch up with me.

I'm staring at the hospital bed void of the mattress and all my stuff I piled on top of it. Probably removed by the cops with all the other missing things after I made them a fire hazard. "This was my bedroom." Uncle Billy and Talia pant softly, inside the doorway now. "Close your eyes."

When I turn to make sure, Uncle Billy has his eyes shut, but Talia's staring at me, the green of her eyes darkened.

"Now picture a boy whose legs don't move, flipped on his stomach, laying on the bed."

I see Uncle Billy nod. When I don't say more right away, I watch Uncle Billy squeeze his eyes shut tighter.

"Move." Out of the corner of my eye, I see Talia take one step toward me. Uncle Billy stays put, rocking on his heels.

"Move." I repeat a little louder, and Talia takes several steps closer. Uncle Billy crosses his arms over his chest, eyes still shut.

"Move!" I yell, and Uncle Billy's eyes dart open as Talia grabs my shoulders and wraps her arms around me from behind. Maybe wanting to hide. Me. Herself. The past.

"What happened?" Billy asks. "What the hell did my brother do to you?"

I gently unwrap my sister's hands and turn my back to Uncle Billy. Lifting my shirt, this time I shut my eyes tightly, fighting back tears.

The sound of metal scraping the floor forces me to look. Uncle Billy is lifting my bed in its entirety from one side, and the whole frame comes to a slamming thud against the nearest wall. Then he marches toward the door, cursing.

"Where you going?" Talia calls out after him.

"Just need to do something." Uncle Billy holds the doorframe, and I hold my breath, thinking he's going to tear it off the wall. "Something I shoulda done a long time ago," Billy says, and my eyes dart between the twisted bed frame and the strong, heaving back of my Dad's younger brother.

I guess the tour is over. Stepping over the mess, I walk up to the mangled bed frame and pull at one of the dislodged, hospital metal bars. "Did you see that?"

We both know the answer to that question.

An unfamiliar feeling washes over me. Not joy. Nor anger. "I think he's gonna kill Dad."

"I hope," Talia says. "Stupid restraining order." And we look at each other. And then laugh out loud.

"Let's jet." I put my arm around my sister's shoulder. "We found what we came here for. And Uncle Billy knows enough of our story. I don't ever wanna see this place again."

I follow my sister down the steps to the kitchen, but the magazine is gone.

"Looking for this?" Uncle Billy's flipping through it by the front door.

"You're still here?" I ask.

"I just needed to make a call." Uncle Billy hands the magazine to Talia, and lifts the fallen family portrait off the ground, leaning it against the wall. "Was that your mother? She was beautiful."

Making our way back into the kitchen, this time Talia leads. And as the three of us sit around the kitchen table, Uncle Billy takes his cowboy hat off, and Talia shares the story of Gita Shah. What she knew of her childhood. What she pieced together of her parents and their lives in India. And then she and I take turns sharing stories we remembered of our years with Mom, leaving out the heartaches. This day has had its share.

"Someday you'll tell me how she passed away?" Uncle Billy says. "Because I want to know that too," and I put my hand over the magazine. Talia covers my hand, and like we're making a secret pact, Uncle Billy covers Talia's hand. But it's no secret. Something happened today. We started out as strangers. Today, we're family.

A knock from the door sounds, and Uncle Billy rises to get it. Talia and I follow, and I'm guessing Lagan's mad worried about my sister. Reggie and Rani probably came with.

Dad stands in the doorway, and Talia pulls out her phone to, I'm sure, dial 911.

I hold my sister's hand down and face Uncle Billy. "Is this some kind of joke? Did you ask him to come here?"

"So you got the grand tour, William," Dad says,

motioning his hand toward the living room.

Uncle Billy slams the front door shut and shoves Dad from behind, pushing him toward the kitchen. One glance at the front door, and I head to the kitchen, Talia on my heels.

"Is it true?" Uncle Billy asks. He's standing between us and Dad, his bulked arms crossed over his chest. "Did you burn your kids? What kind of bloody father does that?"

Dad's smug grin ticks me off. When he reaches and picks up the magazine from the kitchen table and I lunge to intercept, Uncle Billy holds me back.

"I haven't seen this in years." Dad's flipping through the magazine like he's the only one in the room. Then he looks up, moves a step sideways so he can see Talia's face and says, "You know I can't be here. So if it's all right with everyone, my brother and I will carry on this conversation elsewhere," and he starts to walk away, but I push past Uncle Billy.

Blocking Dad's way, I look him in the eye, my open palm in front of me. "Not before you hand it over."

49
~Jesse~

When Dad tries to step around me, I shove him back. Uncle Billy comes from behind and tries to grab the magazine from Dad's hands, but Dad lifts it in the air. "William, now let's not be hasty. I'll show you this back at my place. Let's go now."

Uncle Billy shakes his head, swings back his arm, and punches Dad right in the jaw, Dad's back crashing against the counter, sending the magazine sailing to the kitchen floor. Diving for it first, I land on the floor and Dad jumps on my back, and we scuffle. Kicking and shifting on my stomach, I try to dislodge Dad off my back, but he pins me with his weight. Refusing to move off the magazine and wheezing for air, I manage one word. "Help."

Dad's weight suddenly lifts off me as Uncle Billy picks Dad up, and I flip over to watch Billy slam Dad against the kitchen table. "What the hell, Geri? Pick on someone your own size. What's so special about that issue, Geri?" And then with a voice full of rage, Billy repeats, "Did you or did you not burn your son and your daughter?" making me stumble as I get up off the ground.

"Just taking care of business, little brother. My business. Not yours." Dad's voice sounds like a growl— the growl of an injured tiger.

Talia's standing the furthest away by the kitchen entrance. I move toward her. Uncle Billy raises his chin to me, asking me if there's something I want to say.

"Talia wants it," I say, panting. "It has Mom's picture in it."

"Then it's yours." Uncle Billy turns to Dad and shoves him against the wall again, harder this time. "What's wrong with you?"

Setting the magazine on the kitchen table, I'm frozen with mixed emotions. I want Uncle Billy to keep hitting. But I see my sister wince, and a part of me feels like we're being hit.

"That magazine," Dad says, his jaw jetted out, "Those papers could ruin me, William. They're pictures of women I represented. Women who would say slanderous things about me."

"Women?" I ask.

"Like Jaya?" Talia says. "The woman who died in the car accident? This is about the MOD trial, Dad?"

"So you're a high-profile lawyer who hides evidence?" Uncle Billy's doing the math too.

Dad shakes his head and starts laughing, rises to his feet and then throws his head forward to head-butt Uncle Billy who curses and then swings his right arm back and meets Dad's chest with an upper cut, making Dad buckle over and grip his stomach, gasping for air.

Hearing Dad talk about those women in the magazine returns my own desire to hurt him, but before I can lunge at Dad, Uncle Billy rubs the spot on his forehead, grabs Dad's shoulders, rams him against the side door, and kicks Dad in the gut, sending him to his knees. "That's for burning your kids, you bloody monster."

When Dad starts to rise, fists poised to punch back, Uncle Billy's boot meets Dad's face with a second blow of such force, I see the blood spurt from Dad's mouth. "That's for letting my best friend Joseph die."

And then Uncle Billy lifts Dad by his shoulders, reels him into the oven door, and Dad buckles over the stovetop, moaning. "And that's. For keeping your kids from me."

Seconds later, a low guttural laugh escapes Dad, and Billy shakes his head as he marches closer, flips Dad and pushes him back, one arm pressed on Dad's chest to hold him in place over the stove top. With his free hand, Uncle Billy touches the switch of the burner. Before he turns it on, his eyes meet mine, and when he looks at Talia, her face turned away and her eyes tightly shut, Uncle Billy let's go. Of the switch. And then Dad.

Gasping for air, Dad fumbles to the nearest wall, leans back and slides till he's sitting on the floor, one knee up, blood visible on the edges of his lips.

"Enough." The word leaves Uncle Billy's mouth as he leans against the counter, out of breath. Close enough to pull me forward, Uncle Billy pats my back and mutters, "Strong work," like I'm the one who busted up Dad. He motions for my sister to join us and pulls Talia into a side hug with his other arm.

The pounding on the front door is followed by cops showing up.

"We got a call from the neighbors, reporting some activity in this house. No one's allowed to cross the police tape. You are all under arrest for trespassing."

"But Officer..." I say.

Uncle Billy speaks up. "Sorry sir. This is all my fault."

"Save it for the station," the second cop, a woman,

says.

"I'm from South Africa." Uncle Billy takes a step toward the female officer, his hands open. "And where I come from, you can't be arrested for trespassing in your own house?"

The male cop looks between us and Dad, and calls in to the precinct with his phone, asking about protocol while the woman walks over to Dad. "What about his face? Who beat him up?" She bends down to look Dad in the eye. "What the hell happened to you?"

Dad sputters something incomprehensible, blood covering his teeth and lips, but Uncle Billy clears his throat, directing the officer's attention to my shirt which must have ripped during the scuffle. The air hits my exposed back.

Uncle Billy lifts a ripped corner. "Self-defense, Officer."

"Who did this to you, young man?" The male officer, now off his phone, his hand under Dad's armpit, lifts Dad to his feet, his gaze on me.

Talia responds, "My dad was beating up my brother over a magazine. The magazine might be important evidence."

I reach for the issue on the table. "Let me look at that," the female officer asks, and she takes it from me and starts flipping pages, shaking her head. "I don't know what's going on here, but we'll all go down to the station and sort this out."

And then the other officer gets a call, but he hangs up quickly and forces Dad to turn and face the wall. "For starters, this guy's violated the order of protection against him, and that's enough cause for arrest. You have the right to remain silent…"

As the male officer cuffs Dad, the other cop asks Uncle Billy, "Did you hit him too?" referring to Dad while looking at me. "You have a nice little lump on your forehead."

Uncle Billy rubs the spot where Dad nailed him. "Only did what I needed to do to save the boy. He's like a son to me."

Satisfied, the officer files the magazine into an envelope marked evidence as she reminds us that we still need to come down to the station to give our statements. When I could turn and watch my handcuffed father being led out of the kitchen, I choose to face Uncle Billy instead, soaking in what it feels like to matter to someone. The glint in Uncle Billy's eyes assures me—he meant what he said.

After the officers leave, I walk over to the stove top to test something. "The power's off."

The clicking of the turned switch fails to ignite, and Talia says, "So I was hiding my eyes for nothing," and we all crack up.

When the laughter dies down, Uncle Billy's staring at the teakettle. "So the burns. He really did that to you."

He's not asking as he pulls us both into his arms. And muffled sounds get lost in my shoulder as he says the same two words I said before leaping off the roof. The same two words that have stamped my life for so many days. The words I can finally let go of.

"I'm sorry. I'm sorry. I'm so, so sorry."

50
~Talia~

The road forward hasn't been without its bumps, but like those who followed a star for years in search of a promise, I look up at the night sky, find the brightest star, and remember the gardener's promise to me.

When clouds blanket my world, I imagine holding my breath, diving forward, and swimming through till I find the stars on the other side. Reminding me I'm not alone.

When my feet stumble on stones, I remember the blue heart pendant on my necklace. Looking through it, I know there's a way to see through the past to the future. But the one who laid down his life to build the bridge also gives me the courage to live in the here and now.

Lagan, Reggie and Rani met Uncle Billy at the precinct the day he kicked Dad's butt, and well, that fact alone made him an instant hit. The charges for disregarding the restraining order were dropped since Dad technically showed up second and tried to leave.

As for the magazine, Luke told us that a mutual friend in the D.A.'s Office let it slip that they're investigating the women in the photographs, trying to track them down to find out if any of their stories connect with the trafficking that's suspected to be happening at MOD hotels. It's a long shot, but if even one steps forward, it'll be worth it.

When the new semester kicks off, Rani invites me to share an apartment in downtown Evanston with three other friends. Among other things, I'm excited to learn this Indian cuisine thing together. It's not that different from living in the shelter. The girls in the apartment might not have gone through what I did, but everyone has a story. We'll share them as time goes on. For now, it's nice to have a desk to store my Post-its from Lagan. And a pillow to call my own.

And without asking, Uncle Billy helps me with the rent, new clothes, and books for school. I hang my new wardrobe in the closet after Lagan removes the closet door. Some things just help.

Uncle Billy also covers my tuition, assuring me that he's just trying to make up for all the Christmases and birthdays he missed. The shipping business he's running back home is booming, so he's happy to share with his family, even though Jesse and I are still getting used to the idea that we actually have family.

And he's been teaching Jesse how to drive. There are talks of Jesse going to South Africa, continuing flight lessons over there, maybe learning the ropes of the shipping business, but we have to get through the trial with Dad first.

Sometimes Lagan and I come out to the old garden even if it's only partially open now. We sit on the hood of his dad's car to watch the sunset. And when night comes, we lay back and look for shooting stars. We've

both seen a few. But we have yet to spot the same one.
Just means we have to come back another day.

Jimmy read the news of Dad's arrest and rehires
Jesse right away, giving Jess a chance to save up for
more flight lessons. He also offered Jesse a room to rent
at his mom's place. Uncle Billy offered to pay for his
own place, but Jesse wants to help Amanda, but my little
brother's learning to embrace help, little by little. For
now he's working, reading up on the Air Force, and
spending his spare time with a girl who's addicted to
churros. According to my brother, Summer's happy
Jesse's not leaving any time soon.

Uncle Billy has been running his company via the
Internet, Skyping his girlfriend, and every time we see
each other, he wants to get Chicago-style deep dish,
apparently the best thing he's discovered in America.
Over the past few months, we've also taken a couple of
trips, as a family, to visit Mom's grave in Michigan. And
sometimes when I'm with him and Jesse together, I
think I hear my little brother slip and call him Dad.

Uncle Billy plans to stay until after the trial. That's
what he's decided for now. Luke's thrilled with how I've
progressed in our practice sessions and feels confident
the case will run smoothly. Summer will testify to Jesse's
character even with her family's opposition to
controversy, because she's discovered a kind, generous
dreamer, and she wants everyone to know the man Jesse
is today. Uncle Billy will testify to his brother's past,
what he learned about our abuse, and touch on the loss
of his friend Joseph. And Lagan plans to talk to his and
Rani's parents about what he saw when he was a little
boy, giving the family one more chance to believe Rani's
story.

One day, in early November, on an unusually warm
Chicago day, while out by the Lake with everyone, Uncle

Billy announces, "I'm bringing my girlfriend next month to meet all of you. And check out this crazy Bean."

I tell him, "She'll hate you. Chicago winters are brutal. If you wait till spring, you could take her to the garden. Girls love flowers."

He winks at Lagan and says, "I'll bet whoever wrote that rhyme about two lovers never considered how many couples actually fall in love, sitting in a tree, k-i-s-s-i-n-g."

Heat rushes to my ears as Lagan takes my hand in his and plants a kiss on the back of it. It's a Saturday, and Rani and Reggie have joined us for a stroll around Millennium Park. Jesse walked ahead with Summer. Something about buying a round of churros for everyone.

"So Talia, is it true, you two only slow dance under willow trees?" Uncle Billy's asking.

My face feels hot now too as Lagan says, "That's what you get for telling your uncle all those stories about us." Lagan raises my hand to twirl me, but I resist and play it off like I have a rock in my shoe.

As I'm slipping my boot back on, Jesse returns and passes out brown bags, Summer's lips sprinkled with cinnamon when they join us.

Lagan gets Uncle Billy's attention again with, "Did she mention the time it took like ten Post-its to get her to eat lunch with me?"

"I heard it was twenty." Reggie says, and Rani chimes in, "He told me he got you in three."

"Umm. More like five. Or six at the most." I count in my head to make sure.

Everyone's laughing and Lagan just smiles that heart-stopping smile of his as he continues to bring up the good times, and I can't help but think: This is one of the good times. Right here. Right now.

"Oh, and how 'bout the time she made me dig her a hole in the middle of my parent's backyard just to plant her a willow tree?"

Wait, what? I let go of Lagan's hand and wave to get my Uncle's attention. "Now that, I'm pretty sure, if it happened, happened in his dreams."

Lagan takes my hand and leads me to the park with brass figures, some standing facing each other. Some sitting on a park bench and then he stops in front of two figures kneeling in the dirt. Our friends and family follow.

"What's going on?" I say, glancing back, but no one's saying anything. Everyone's munching on churros, seeming to wait on Lagan for an explanation.

We're inches from the two figures on their knees.

"I asked the city for permission to plant a willow tree here, and they said, yes." Lagan takes my hand and I follow his lead as he kneels next to the figures. "But one condition, when the garden opens in the spring, they'll help us to transplant it. Since that's where it belongs. Home."

I notice the small bump in the dirt. That must be where Lagan planted the seed, and as I bend down to touch it, he says, "Oh, I picked the spot and spent yesterday morning breaking through the ground. But I want us to plant it together." He pauses and Reggie gives him a hand shovel from his backpack. "According to what I read on line, the seed has to be six inches deep and watered every day if we want this new life to grow." Lagan glances up at our friends and family. "That's where all of you can help."

From the smiles on their faces, everyone seems on board. I guess we'll come up with a schedule.

"Wow. What a sweet idea," I say, although words can't adequately express how special this all feels.

"Want to the honors?" Lagan hands me the little hand shovel and I dig up some dirt. Then he takes it and digs some more, and as we make a small pile of earth next to us, I recall the first time he saw me covered with dirt under our willow. He called me beautiful.

We're still digging when Lagan leans forward and says, "Did you know that the bark of a willow tree has anti-inflammatory properties?"

I'm tempted to laugh out loud. Someone's been doing his research. The words repeat in my head. One part repeats loudest. Anti-inflammatory. Maybe that means something specific to doctors. To me, it means to put a flame out. With so many storms fought, it's a miracle our willow's roots survived. I'm guessing Lagan knows. It might be a while till we see any signs of life at the garden, outside the greenhouse, but it helps to know there's hope. Because hope, well, it changes everything.

"I think that's good," Lagan says, putting the shovel aside and fishing a three-inch-square brown box out of his sweatshirt pocket and handing it to me.

Popping off the lid, a Post-it Note lies on top, and I can't help but giggle.

It reads: Can I plant a kiss on you? But first…

Glancing up at Lagan, his dimple is like the dot on an exclamation point. He's enjoying every second of this.

"Does the next box have a blue tulip bulb in it?" Tulips. Two lips. I didn't forget.

As I lift the Post-it to pick out the seed, something sparkles underneath. Something green. And also blue.

My hand covers my mouth when I notice Lagan. He's kneeling on one knee as he takes my hand in his.

"Some people make wishes when they see a falling star. Or when they blow out a candle. Not me. I made one wish when I met you, Dewdrop. That someday you'd trust me. Will you trust me, Talia? Not today. Not tomorrow. But someday, when you're ready, will you marry me?"

I'm nodding over and over again as Lagan takes the heart-shaped, emerald-sapphire, silver band out of the box and slides it on my ring finger, and cheers from behind fill the air.

"To forever." Lagan whispers in my ear as he helps me to rise to my feet, hugging me tightly. "To our forever."

And Jesse comes in to hug me, giving Lagan a high five, and Reggie follows with a chest to chest and a "You did it man! You rock!"

Rani hugs us both too, pretending to wipe away tears, and saying, "My little cousin's all grown up."

Summer smiles, and I invite her into our circle of hugs, and she comes, pretty in her pink sweater dress and black winter boots. Pretty as always.

Uncle Billy's clapping, but he hasn't moved closer. I let go of Lagan's hand and approach him. "I'm really glad you're here," I say.

"Thanks for sharing this day with me," he says. "So glad I found you and Jesse. For all the wrong your Dad did, one thing he did right was help me to find you. And look at you. You're all grown up. About to get married someday. So glad I didn't miss this."

Lagan shakes Uncle Billy's hand as he congratulates him on a job well done. I watch my Uncle's expression as he turns to Jesse and asks, "And when might you plant a tree with Summer?"

But Jesse just punches Uncle Billy in the arm.

"My parents and sis are waiting for us to celebrate." Lagan directs us downtown toward a restaurant he picked out.

When the light turns red at the crosswalk, I lean over

and kiss my Post-it Prince.

A few passing cars honk their approval.

And as we walk across the street, I can't help but ask, "So about the tree…"

"There's no tree," Lagan says, shrugging his shoulders. "It was just a distraction to surprise you."

"But there could be? Right? I mean, every willow started out a seed, right?"

"Correct." Lagan's dimple lights up. "And every waterfall starts out with one drop. Like a dewdrop. Dance with me."

And he lifts one hand and I let him twirl me. I'm holding on. Trusting.

EPILOGUE
~Talia~

The courthouse steps lie before me, as inviting as
Lagan's proposal. Maybe more. I've waited for this day
my whole life. And with each step, I think of all the
people I love. Each star in my sky. Each person I will
speak for today when it's my turn on the witness stand.

For Jaya. Because no one should ever have to live in
a house colored black all the days of her life.

For Jesse. Because my little brother learned to walk
again. Live again. And now care about someone.

For Lagan. For gifting me kindness in Post-it sized
portions. And for not giving up on me when I wanted to
give up on myself.

And for Mom. For all the hits you took in our place.
For how long you braved the storms and for trying to
get us out, even if we were caught. You tried. I know
you loved us. You were the star the gardener planted in
my sky the day I was born. You were my falling star the
day you breathed your last. I'm sorry your light turned
off before this day. More than anyone, this day is for
you.

"Talia Grace Vanderbilt." The clerk says my name,

239

holding a book in front of me. *The Beautiful Fight.*

Yes, I whisper inside me to the gardener as I raise my right hand. It sure has been. One long, hard, and beautiful fight.

"Do you swear to tell the truth, the whole truth, and nothing but the truth?"

I've lived in the in between. Between what if and what is. Between yesterday and forever. Between holding and letting go.

Glancing at Lagan, Jesse, and lastly, Dad, I clear my throat and voice my answer. "I do."

ACKNOWLEDGEMENTS

To my husband, Santhosh. Where do I begin? These past few months have been some of the toughest we've faced with the news of your heart and the loss of your dad, Appa. I don't want to imagine what life would be like without you next to me. So I won't. Instead, I strive to treasure each day, each moment, and every heartbeat that God gives us to be together. Like I said on New Year's Eve, stealing from one of my favorite songs by Smokey Robinson, "Let's take it one heartbeat…at a time." Love you so much, Sunshine.

Thank you Mom and Dad, especially during this season when we needed a few extra hugs. You always deliver. Thank you Amma for being my mom when my own mom was not nearby. Appa- thank you for accepting me as your own daughter seventeen years ago. I'll never forget you.

To my baby sis, Sandi. Thank you for your example of courage in my life. And your voice of motivation that never gives up on me. Can't believe your first prince is going off to college this year! So excited for Nesean!

To my brothers and sisters: Suresh, Celine, Zulima, Arul & Tracy. I can't imagine going through life without all of you by my side. Maybe the law made us siblings, but the love you show to hubby and me makes us family. I treasure you all.

To my super talented niece, Deepa. Thanks for all your hard work on the cover of Soaring Through Stars. I never doubted for a moment that you would make it shine! To all my nieces and nephews: thanks for reading my stories and sharing them with your friends.

To my best friend, Roopa. Thank you for being my first reader. Like a great book, we can pick up where we left off, even if we haven't talked in a while. Your love and encouragement are priceless.

To my dear friend and lawyer, Linda from Chicago. Thanks so much for all your lawyerly advice on the courtroom scenes. And also my friend and judge, Tim Driscoll, thank you for talking through a few key details during the final edits.

To my friends and neighbors. You have been my family and cheered me on every step of the way, and words cannot express how much I value you.

To all my writing buds, my street teamers, and in my crit group. Thank you for spurring me on, reading early drafts, and making me a better writer.

To Chris for helping me with the flight school scene. Your notes were invaluable, and I never tire of seeing your cloud-filled pictures on Facebook.

To Shaun, my South African ambassador. Thanks for taking the time to make Uncle Billy sound real. I hope someday I get to visit your beautiful country.

To my editor, Beth Jusino. So sweet to finally share a cuppa (or two) in Seattle, laugh together, and connect face to face, Beth. You have pushed me further than any English teacher I ever had to find the best journey for my characters. I appreciate your investment in my fictional worlds. And my real world too.

To my line editor, Hwee, thanks for dotting my i's and crossing my t's.

To my agent, Chip Macgregor. I love talking books and story ideas with you. Glad you're on my side, Chip.

To my readers. I know affirmation isn't everything. But it's a pretty huge something. And your Likes, Tweets, Facebook comments, and Amazon Reviews make a huge difference in the confidence of this newbie writer. Thank you from the bottom of my heart to the top of my waterfalls for buying, reading, and sharing my books. Hugs. And more hugs.

Finally, I want to thank God for waking me up every day and giving me the coolest job in the world—making up stories to share what matters to me most. Grace.

ABOUT THE AUTHOR

Rajdeep decided to be a writer during her junior year in high school after her English teacher gave her an "F" but told her she had potential. She studied English Literature at Northwestern University, and she writes Masala-marinated, Young Adult Fiction, and blogs at rajdeeppaulus.com.

When Paulus is not tapping on her Mac, you can find her dancing with her four princesses, kayaking with her hubs, coaching basketball or eating dark chocolate while sipping a frothy, sugar-free latte. Find her on Twitter, Instagram, Tumbler, Goodreads, and Pinterest @rajdeeppaulus.

OMGosh! It's over. What do I do now?

You read the trilogy and like a long but A-Mazing vacation, it's finished. Time to pack up and go home.

BUT WAIT! I have a few ideas how you can manage your book-over. If you like. If you want to know more. Do more. Be more. ☺

Suggestions are, and not limited to, the few listed below:

1. Pop over to my bloggity Blog **rajdeeppaulus.com** and peruse the madness of my daily life or search Fiction Friday for some short stories. Free. YES. FREE STUFF!

2. Find me on **Wattpad**. I have a Work In Progress called, Crush Me that I'm about ten-ish chapters in. Read it and let me know what you think so far. It's FREE. YES. More Free stuff!

3. Find me on **Social Media** and say hello. And ask me a question about what I didn't get a chance to address in the books. I'll do my best to respond. So yes. I'm looking forward to meeting you.

4. Share a short review on **Amazon** or **Goodreads**. It means SO MUCH to hear your honest feedback, and it also BIGTIME helps other readers to find a new book.

5. Invest in someone like Talia or Jesse. Support organizations that aid survivors of human trafficking like **Nomi Network**, **World Vision** or **Cycling for Change**. Be the change you dream of.

xo - raj